I0783257

In One Life and Out Another

J. Mercer

Bare Ink

Published 2023 / Bare Ink

Printed in the United States of America

Hardcover ISBN: 979-8-9872567-2-5

E-ISBN: 979-8-9872567-1-8

Paperback ISBN: 979-8-9872567-3-2

Library of Congress Control Number: 2023901338

IN ONE LIFE AND OUT ANOTHER / written by J Mercer

Cover designs by Robin Vuchnich

Copy edits by Erika Manternach

Contents

Before...

I HAD A PICTURE from the day my life split. I did my best not to look at it.

The grass was an intense green behind us, and we held half-eaten ice cream cones in our hands. Hannah's perfect teeth matched her wide smile and endless wavy mane, while Whitney's short smile emphasized her round mouth and blunt bob. My grin was pressed thin, and my hair was back in a messy bun, the finer strands loose around my face—boy catchers, my dance teacher called them. Though, at that point, it had only been Hannah who'd caught any boys.

"What's the plan for tomorrow?" Whit had asked, right after Hannah took the picture.

"The mall," Hannah decided, because she did most of the deciding.

"Don't we always go to the park on Marin's birthday?"

"It's fine," I said, as my parents' voices lifted out our open windows on wings of fighter jets. We were two full houses away.

"Is that your dad?" Hannah asked. Surprised, because my dad was a comfortable pile of big feet and wandering thoughts. He did not raise his voice.

At the subsequent howl, Whitney muttered, "That's definitely your mom." My mom won all tournaments in the art of theatrics.

"Do you think something happened?" I asked, my mind scanning the scattered relatives who could've gone extinct. Except, my parents wouldn't be screaming at each other if someone had died, wouldn't be throwing bombs and land mines—*you never* and *I always* and *how dare you!*

"Stay here, okay?" I told Hannah and Whitney. "I'll be right back." Then I raced the rest of the way home, flew up the steps, and slammed every window shut.

The most unsettling thing about this was that my parents didn't fight. They spent most of their time doing the very opposite of that, which was not talking at all. It led me to wonder what the screaming meant—were they finally going to put each other out of their misery and get a divorce, or was this the start of them working things out?

There is a story that lays a course of two roads
diverged in a yellow wood. If you ride to the
left, you'll lose your horse, but to the right it
will be your head.

— Robert Frost/Russian folk tale mashup

Chapter 1

Either divorce...

I HAD MY OWN car. A moving vehicle. A medium of freedom.

No longer was I stranded at my mom's on her nights. No longer could she tell me she wasn't comfortable with me driving her car, or complain about the wear and tear, or bug me to play a game of *Scrabble*.

I was finally seventeen. Freedom wasn't too much to ask.

The first place we went was the mall. Hannah was shopping for a romantic comedy—she themed our mall excursions this way—and I was buying myself a birthday gift.

Dad had been the main force behind the car, and my mom had gotten me all her favorite things: a new yoga mat, citrus-blend essential oil, and a worry stone.

Hannah nudged me while I paid for the lavender *eau de toilette* I'd asked for, and as I glanced up, her eyes and head directed me toward the display a few feet away. Our ex-BFF Whitney was there, fingering a headband, her back to us.

She was so strange these days, and always by herself.

Once in a while, she had a boy with her—weird-looking older boys with long hair and pinched faces. Boys, and sometimes her little sister, but no friends. I never saw her with a friend.

Slipping a headband under her sweatshirt, Whitney snuck out of the store. Hannah followed while I grabbed my bag and change from the cashier.

"Can you believe that?" Hannah muttered as I caught up.

"She's never worn a headband in her life," I agreed. Because they hurt her ears.

"She hardly washes her hair."

The platinum blonde did make even Whitney's pale roots seem clogged with dust and dirt, but it worked for her. Besides, our past should count for something.

Hannah took one look at my face and looped her arm through mine. "Calm down. You know I'm not serious."

I could see from where we were, maybe ten paces behind Whitney, that she was hugging herself as she walked. She was also hunched over, and the only times I remembered her standing like that were when she was sad. "Maybe we should ask her to eat lunch with us."

"I thought we were having ice cream."

We used to bike to the old drugstore, back when we were still friends. Claustrophobic and stacked tight with all sorts of things, its shining beacon was the soft-serve machine. Hannah and I built the tallest cones we could, while Whitney bought up all the weird, old candy. Then we'd sit on the lawn of the ancient stone library across the street.

"For old time's sake," I said. "Since it's my birthday."

Letting go of me, Hannah pranced a few steps forward. "Hey, Whit!" Cue Hannah's trademark smile: big, bold, and convincing.

Whitney slowed and looked back, but as soon as she registered us, she kept walking.

Right. You can't drop someone like a bad itch first day of freshman year and then have lunch like nothing happened three years later.

Hannah caught up and grabbed Whitney's baggy gray hoodie, causing Whit to spin around with a sneer. Hannah let go like she'd been bitten and took a step back.

"It's Marin's birthday," Hannah said. "She just got a car and we're celebrating with ice cream."

I waited for Hannah to add that Whitney was invited, but since she didn't, it only felt like she was rubbing it in. "Do you want to come?" I asked.

Hannah frowned, even though I'd said we should ask her. "Remember our drugstore?"

Whitney shifted her attention back and forth between us, then settled narrowed eyes on Hannah. "No."

"Yes, you do. How can you not remember our drug-store?"

"No, I don't want to have lunch with you."

Hannah shrugged and looped her arm through mine to

pull me away. But I felt rooted, like I'd slid back into some sort of mold I'd forgotten I belonged to. My feet didn't budge.

Whitney brought her unsettling look my way. It whispered, *I know who you are, and I don't like it.* "Maybe Marin should be in charge on her birthday," she said. And then she was off, weaving into a family as they walked by so we couldn't catch her again.

Stalking over to the bank of gumball machines, Hannah put a coin in. "You're in charge on your birthday. What's she talking about?"

"Well, I did want tacos for lunch," I pointed out.

"Tacos are boring."

"American tacos, maybe, but not real tacos." I took the gumball from her, and she got another for herself. She might make all the decisions, but she did give me the first of everything.

The second gumball dropped out of her hand, onto the floor, and she spun to set her butt against the gumball display, holding onto it for support.

"Are you okay?" I mumbled over the freshly chewed gum in my mouth. "Hannah?"

"Gray," she muttered, eyes on the floor, then to my shirt. "Green."

She'd been having these panic attacks lately, and the therapist told her to count colors. Whatever that meant. It was supposed to distract her from her anxiety and keep her focused on the present. She reached for me, and I held her hand, then also her chin, keeping her eyes on mine and breathing with her, an even and steady in and out. "Brown," she muttered at my freckles. "Brown," to my hair. "Flesh of a Scandinavian."

I laughed, which got a twitch of a smile out of her. "Maybe you should be counting gumball colors instead."

She sucked in air like it was a fight, each breath, and I wondered for the millionth time if an inhaler would help. But the doctors said nothing was wrong with her lungs.

"I'm thinking you can reach six inches today," I told her, speaking of our upcoming ice cream cones. "A new world record." Hannah was an expert with the soft-serve machine. Eighty-nine cents per cone but no height limit meant once you got the technique right, you were golden.

Hannah was pretty much always golden, from the tips of her shiny hair to the soles of her designer shoes, so it made sense she could work this trick like no one else. I'd tried and given up, and now she made mine, too.

Distraction seemed to help the most, and soon she'd bustled past this episode like it had never happened. Honestly, I think they bothered me more than they bothered her.

"Whitney is missing out," she muttered, an hour later, as she handed me my four inches. Always four for me. Sky was the limit for her.

"As if you're surprised." I reconciled our vanished

friendship with the fact that Whitney had refused to try out for dance team. We'd been swallowed up by it, and it was a pretty tight group. Our new friends could never understand Whit's prickly outside.

"I could make her over into something spectacular," she said, as she got into position. She had to concentrate if she wanted to stretch the limit. This meant feet out to brace herself, head bent forward like a chicken, lips parted, teeth clamped down on her tongue.

"She doesn't need a makeover." Whitney wasn't sparkly and clean like Hannah and me, but the dark eyes worked for her, the ripped jeans, the hair.

Hannah raised a dubious eyebrow in my direction. It was enough of a distraction to mess with the ice cream's delicate balance, which meant she had to stop now or risk it toppling over. She groaned.

"Sorry," I said. "I'll eat two. You can try again."

She waved a hand in the air. "It's fine. Sam's last girl-friend was a stick. Maybe less ice cream will slim my natural curves."

Sam.

"I thought you gave up on him last year." I tried to act normal, tried not to hold my breath, tried not to remind her that he had very clearly said *no, thank you.* Tried not to let on how badly I wanted him myself—though this was something she should already know.

She shrugged and dropped two dollars down on the

counter, while her tongue snaked out to lick the side of her cone. "He's still my all-time favorite."

"Hi, ladies," said the 200-year-old pharmacist with the perfect ice cream formula. "Nice to see you again, controlling yourselves."

Hannah nodded toward me. "She controls herself. I try not to."

"This isn't your best work, though," he noted, as he rang us up.

Pocketing the change, she whispered, "Marin distracted me."

"It's always my fault," I added.

"Pretty much." She winked, but neither of us could tell if that was for him or for me. It was one of her talents, making everyone feel like her attention was only on them. At the front of the store, she pushed the door open with the back of her shoulder. "Want to come over for dinner?"

"Yes, but I can't." My mom was making me dinner, and missing too many of those wasn't worth the subsequent theatrics. Not to mention, it was my birthday. No way I could avoid her all day and not live to regret it.

"You know," Hannah said, as I unlocked the car and she slid into her seat, "when we're at KU, you can come for dinner all you want, and your mom will never have to know you're in town." The University of Kansas was her first choice, a horrifying half hour away. But it meant I would be too accessible. My mom could literally show up at our dorm without warning.

"Wash U, you mean?" This was my reach school, my ultimate goal—still in-state but a four-hour drive, which meant plenty of breathing room. The problem was, it was private, and my dad was only paying the equivalent of in-state, public-school tuition.

She rolled her eyes because she didn't have the grades for Wash U. "Go Wildcats!" she muttered, referring to K-State, our compromise. Two hours away.

Hannah finished her cone while I turned into the residential area connecting our two neighborhoods, and I finished mine as I dropped her off.

Though I knew her about as well as I knew anyone, I still couldn't wrap my mind around her not wanting to leave for college. Even though Kansas City was pretty great, and even though stepping into her house felt like a soft pillow, a cozy blanket, and a warm fire, all cocooned in a safety net, what about seeing the world? Even if it was just another city in the same state. Anything to get out of the cage that was my life.

The closer I got to my mom's, the more I felt like I was underwater and fighting a riptide—the drag, the pull, the leeching of my soul seeping out of me.

My mom cornered me in the tiny foyer when I walked in, an oven mitt on one hand and her dark bangs split like she'd been messing with them too much. "Where've you been?" she asked, not moving to let me into the living room.

"With Hannah."

"Sundays are mine, Marin. Not Hannah's." Spinning around, she headed for the kitchen.

My mom seemed to think she was the only person I should spend time with during her joint-custody hours. She figured if she lived with me all the time, she'd get half my life, so since she had me only half my life, she should get it all to herself.

Point one of contention.

Fishing my phone out of my backpack, I slumped down on the plump couch, which about swallowed me whole, and took a deep breath of spaghetti sauce.

Popping my earbuds in, I closed my eyes and let my mind run through the pom choreography Hannah and I had been working on earlier that morning.

My name, distant, and a rap to my knee. My mom, standing over me, taking my earbud out. "Are you only here for food?"

Point two of contention: she didn't believe I wanted to spend time with her.

This hadn't always been true, but if you perpetually whimper about something like that, it does turn itself into a self-fulfilling prophecy. Even so, the guilt stretched taut in my gut, tangling veins with clawed nails.

She turned to the kitchen. "Come set the table. Come talk to me."

"About what?" But I followed her.

"Anything." She handed me the napkins she'd already pulled out and the silverware she'd set on top of them. "How was your day?"

"Good."

"You and Hannah ready for cuts?"

"We're front-and-center in the formation, Mom. We're the ones doing the choreography."

"Right, of course, such a big shot now."

Not only had I shown her the practice video, but I'd told her I'd made choreo committee. She knew what that meant. Had she been paying any attention at all?

"Surely you didn't practice all day."

"We went to the mall."

"And?"

"Had ice cream for lunch."

"You skipped lunch?"

"I ate a late breakfast."

"What'd you eat for breakfast?"

"Brownies." All my mom thought my dad fed me was dessert. I'd actually had granola with bananas and milk. Three whole food groups, thank you very much.

"That doesn't sound very nutritious, Marin."

"I wasn't aiming for nutritious."

"Dancers can't be flippant about nutrition."

"I know, Mom."

"As athletes, we have to feed our bodies enough energy

to equal the output we demand of them."

"I know, Mom."

"Not to mention, you get used to eating all that stuff and when you get old, your metabolism slows down and then you end up like your father."

I raised an eyebrow. My dad had maybe five percent more body fat than she did.

Mom served up dinner—an extra-large salad for me—then proceeded to tell me about all the vitamins and minerals each item contained. Why I needed them and how much I needed, broken down by hour of dance. I tried to keep my mouth as full as possible so I'd appear incapable of carrying on half of this exhausting conversation.

The difference between my mom's for dinner versus my dad's for breakfast was stark. He chewed more than he talked. He harped at me about nothing and assumed I could make my own decisions without acute oversight.

To one, an adult; to the other, a toddler. This was my split personality.

My split life.

Chapter 2

...or not.

I HAD MY OWN car. A moving vehicle. A medium of freedom.

No longer did I have to fight my mom to use hers, sneak out with my dad's when she wasn't watching, or beg a ride off Whit's boyfriends.

The first place we went, of course, was the park. We had our own bench there. Surrounded by trees, it was hidden from all three playgrounds and propped in front of the running trail that wound along the creek. In case anyone got any ideas, we'd carved our names into it, along with the initials of all the boys we'd ever liked and a tally of our petty crimes against humanity, a reminder of what we had to make up for. Mostly, I stole little things from my mom, like gum and socks, while Whitney grabbed hair accessories for her younger sister. Either way, they counted the same as breaking a heart or lying to a teacher.

Today, in honor of me getting my actual, very own car, Whitney had stolen a pack of her father's cigarettes. She lit me one, and the first drag nearly sent me into convulsions.

"We really need to get ourselves a vape."

"For my eighteenth birthday, I'll buy you one."

"For your eighteenth birthday, I'll buy *you* one. You'll have to buy it, of course, but I'll get you the money."

The pounding of feet grew obvious from beyond the trees. We focused our attention that way, straightening up and curling our legs under the seat, hands braced on the bench.

As soon as he came into sight, I started with the stats, golf-announcer style: "Lone male. Thirty-four years old. Six three, one-hundred-ninety-nine pounds. Breathing: moderate. Pretty good for mile three. Running to keep hot for his wife, a curvy redhead who has a wandering eye. Oh wait, breaking news: that's his mistress he's running for. Sorry, folks. Correction: mistress."

"Lookin' good, baby!" Whit cried out. "Keep it up!" This was punctuated with an ear-deafening whistle.

He batted a hand in our direction but didn't look our way. We hadn't figured out if that was supposed to be a wave or a screw-you. He'd done it every time, except for the first, when he'd completely ignored us and our laughter.

As soon as he was out of sight, Whit let out a dramatic sigh. "Kyle and I broke up."

"Yeah?" It wasn't much of a surprise, but I had to play like it was. No need to get into why all her relationships fizzled out. She never took it well.

"He said I was suffocating him." She sneered. "Didn't

mind it so much when I was naked, but want to spend one night out in the world and that's too much."

"What did you even like about him, though?" I asked. My angle was to obtusely remind her she didn't have very high standards in the hopes she'd realize she didn't have to go out with everyone who looked her way.

Whit picked at her thumbnail, which was so short it hurt to look at. "He's hot. I liked his arms."

I held back from telling her that he wasn't hot at all. He was mangy and hardly washed himself. I wouldn't have touched him with the lit end of a cigarette. "Arms are temporary. Brains aren't." I grabbed her hand to make her stop ripping up her cuticles. "Who's next?" Because if she didn't focus on that, she'd end up back with Kyle as soon as he was horny enough to have another go at her.

Shaking me off, she started playing with her hair. It was straight as blades and currently fell past her shoulders. "Anyone with a car. At least until I can drive myself."

Whit was an awful driver and couldn't pass the test for the life of her. She was on a hiatus of even attempting it at this point. I tried not to make a face at the kind of boys she might end up with if her only criteria were *interested in sex* and *has a car.*

I grabbed at the pack she was pounding a cigarette out of and got myself another. We settled back in our seats, taking lazy drags and waiting for the next unsuspecting runner to come by. Though, like the last guy, they weren't always so unsuspecting. In fact, the next one was a regular, too, and he'd taken to whistling at us before we had a chance to whistle at him. For him, we'd taken to dramatic swooning instead of our normal play-by-play.

"Maybe he's who I need," Whit muttered, watching his back as it disappeared.

I snorted. "He's, like, fifty."

She straightened in her seat. "Thirty at the most."

"*No.*" I shook my head, serious now. "Please tell me you're joking."

Blinking away her thoughts, she shrugged. "My dad thinks I need more maturity in my life." I gaped at her. She grinned. "Maybe I'll have to take up running."

Before I could form words in protest, we got distracted by another runner. Two more and a speed walker later, we were back at my car, and Whit was presenting me with a bottle of *eau de toilette*. "It's softer than perfume, and fancier."

"How is *toilet water* fancier than perfume?"

"Because it's French. Anyway, we should keep it in your glovebox for when we need to cover our scent."

"I'd just say I was at your house. And your dad will never be able to tell the difference."

She spritzed me anyway, front and back, then did herself. Sliding into the passenger seat, she secured the bottle in the glove compartment. The lavender clung to me, sinking deep into pores I didn't know I had.

Resting her arm on the open window, she drummed her fingers to the beat of the music as I drove the four blocks to our favorite drugstore. I parked on the curb, behind Sam Hanson's truck.

Whit opened the door to an old-fashioned jingle and elbowed me as she caught sight of him. I elbowed her back as he glanced over from the ice cream machine.

Hannah was mid-build.

Her ice cream cones had been epic, back when we were still friends. Knowing her, they were probably even more epic now. She grew, it's what she did. She always had, gotten bigger and bigger every year, not only taller like the rest of us, but by collecting adjectives. First she was bright, then charming, then contagious, only to finally settle at a blinding sun. Or at least, that's when I'd stopped paying attention.

Sam noticed me and spun with a grin, knocking into her.

"Ugh!" she groaned. "Sam, look what you did. This one could have been the Eiffel Tower."

"You work this weekend?" he asked me.

"Yes." Slipping into the candy aisle, I ran my fingers over the dusty shelves. The dust was part of the charm, like we'd really been transported to a past century, before big chains with glossy tiles and bright UFO lights.

"He wants to work with you," Whitney whispered, elbowing me again.

I gave her a look. She winked at me and carried on. Root

beer candy, butterscotch, spice drops, those weird bumpy balls that made me shiver just looking at them.

Sam's round head peeked into the aisle. "What days?"

"Sam," Hannah's voice snapped. "Get back here and tell me how much ice cream you want."

Sam ignored her, and as the rest of him emerged in the aisle, I walked toward him and leaned against the pale metal shelves. Hannah appeared behind him.

"Is this good?" she asked, a hand outstretched between us. It looked like she was offering him a cone but felt like she was blocking an electric current. Squinting, I could even imagine the frizz as it shook through her hair.

I pulled a dollar out of my pocket to trade her for the ice cream. "It's been a while, Hannah. Thank you."

"That wasn't for you, Marin," she said, even though she'd let me take it.

"I know, but I wanted it."

"You can't just take whatever you want."

I snorted, because irony. "Don't worry. I don't think we want the same things." She wanted Sam's heart forever, and I just wanted to enjoy him as he was, from afar.

With a sneer, she ripped the dollar out of my hand and spun away.

"Seriously, Marin." Sam put a finger to the shelf and wrote an *M* in the layer of dust. "When will I see you?"

I shrugged. "This weekend."

"Come on, Sam. We're leaving." His bald friend reached

a thick fist out and yanked him away into the desert that surrounded Hannah's cold, dead heart. It was the oasis in her that people were drawn to, that they braved the sandstorms for. A drink from that oasis was life-giving, if you could get over the rest of it.

"Delicious," Whit muttered in my ear.

"Sam?"

"No. You trying to pretend you don't want to wrap him up and put him in your pocket."

"Oh, shut up." I took the biggest mouthful of ice cream I could.

"What are the odds you'd end up liking the only boy Hannah couldn't get?"

"Maybe that's *why* I like him. Because he's the only one smart enough to resist her. But I don't like him, not like that."

"Right. And I could live without candy." Brushing past me with about two armfuls of the stuff, she swayed to the counter and let it fall across the surface like an avalanche.

Ernie, the should-be-retired pharmacist who owned the store, grinned with all his fine, fake teeth. "Nicely done. Always topping yourself."

Whit held her arms out. "The bigger I get, the more I can carry."

He chuckled and rang her up. Since his candy was probably decades old, his prices were unreasonably low, and he handed out free lollies to all his customers, even those who were already buying boatloads of sugar. I passed, seeing as I was still working on the cone, but Whitney would never.

She sucked on that lolly, tighter and tighter, the closer we got to her house. I felt it, too. Hannah's place, unlike either of ours, had been comfortable, always light and airy with a breeze. We'd spent pretty much all our time there, until she kicked us out.

Her ice cream cones, the oasis, and her house—that's what I missed about Hannah.

Whitney didn't say anything as she got out of my car, just marched up and in, armed with sugar.

I, on the other hand, drove underwater the rest of my way home. Like a Band-Aid, though, once I was in the driveway, I ran in and got it over with.

I could hear the rumble of the television from the living room, where my dad was no doubt avoiding my mom, and my mom stood at the stove, head down and hair swept over one shoulder. She didn't look up at me. "Could you please set the table."

It was amazing how she could turn questions into statements. I found it pretty impossible to ask a question, especially one that contained a please, and not have my voice curl up at the end.

Pulling the plates from the shelf with one hand, I slid open the silverware drawer with the other. Counting out three forks and three napkins, I dumped it all on the table. Drinks would come later.

Without a glance at her, I tried to slip into the hall.

"Not so fast, Marin." She motioned me over. "Come stir for me."

Everything seemed in order. The glacier gray countertops were clean and the dishes stacked nicely in the gaping dishwasher. Her bamboo cutting board was clear, no vegetables waiting their turn. She offered me the tasting spoon, and I slurped a bit off.

"Does it need more basil?" she asked.

I shook my head. "It's sublime." I did love my mom for her food.

Swiping the leftover with her finger, she sucked on it, rocking her head back and forth. Then added more basil.

"Where've you been," she asked, but disguised as another statement.

"You didn't track me?"

"I only do that after dark."

I let out a single laugh, not that I was amused. "I was with Whitney."

"I didn't ask who, I asked where."

"The park."

"What would two respectable seventeen-year-old girls be doing at the park?"

I tilted my head over the steam, the tomatoes and garlic lingering with the lavender and boiling my surface numb. A numb surface was a handy thing to have. "Well, clearly we're not respectable."

She didn't reply right away, and I could almost feel her measuring and assessing. Then, "I always start out nice and you have to turn it ugly."

"You started out nice?" Nice was lacing a snotty question with a snide tone to imply that your daughter was hooking or buying drugs at the park?

"Must you be mean to me? I've had a long day, Marin."

"You're the one being bitchy about the park."

"I might be bitchy sometimes, but at least I'm not a bitch all the time."

Her words clogged my throat, not that I hadn't heard them before. I dropped the spoon in the pot. "I'm happy to banish myself to my room so I don't further ruin your evening."

"You will be at dinner, even if you ruin it." She grabbed for the spoon, her stirring now jerky and agitated.

Yeah, well, I was jerky and agitated, too. But the brilliant thing was that now I had a car. I could get out. I could speed down the highway and drive until I was bleeding from my eyes. That, or I could stay for the fight.

It was a choice now, at least, where before, I'd been a caged animal, forced into the ring.

I headed for the back door, biting down a smile as she yelled after me to *get back here right now, I don't know where the hell you think you're going.*

She wanted a fight? Fine. I was always ready for a fight.

Chapter 3
Either high school dance...

HANNAH AND I WERE trying not to critique the freshmen's pom technique too loudly as we came out of the locker room. It wasn't their fault—they were just learning—but Hannah thought they were wasting our time.

"Dance is a competitive sport," she was reiterating. "If you can't get the tricks and the choreo, you shouldn't be here."

"They're babies," I countered. "We didn't know pom technique before our freshman year, either."

"Survival of the fittest, Marin."

I raised an eyebrow at her because she'd nearly fainted in there. Said something about not eating lunch and a migraine setting in. I'd had to run across the school to the lunchroom to grab a bag of chips and a soda from the machines. She probably shouldn't be talking about survival of the fittest.

She waved my look off as if it was nothing, and to cheer her up, I started singing the song we'd just watched thirty girls dance to, which was, in fact, about surviving. Turning the corner into the cafeteria, I let loose the high note, which then slid out from under me as I spotted Sam. He was on a bench, gym bag at his feet and hands tangled around the straps like he was waiting for someone. Even sweaty after soccer practice, he could flip my stomach.

"Hey, Marin." His voice was deep and gravelly, but in the best way.

"Hey, Sam." This was nothing new. His friends were our friends, and our friends were his friends.

He stood. "You drive today?"

I shook my head that I hadn't. Both my parents lived a few blocks away, so I only drove when the weather was crappy. My mom had been drilling it into my head since I was little: we walked wherever we could, took the stairs when available, and parked as far as the lot would allow. All these little things, she insisted, would add up to your daily allotment of physical activity.

My mom was big on daily allotments.

"Want a ride home?" he asked.

"Oh, um..."

A frown skipped across Hannah's face, but in her recovery, she grinned large. "We'd love one."

Sam looked back and forth between us, but Hannah kept her smile bright. He finally responded, "Okay?"

"Now, Sam," Hannah said, spinning his name out slowly like cotton candy. "Don't make this a hit to my ego, huh?"

"I wasn't aware your ego was vulnerable in any way." He

threw the bag over his shoulder and stood there as if he was waiting for me to walk with him. Hannah's face... It was directed at him, but it was furrowed. And she only furrowed when she was caught off guard.

Hannah was seldom caught off guard.

Then again, I normally told her everything.

My stomach curled as I fell into step next to him, and I focused on our feet as he held the door open for me.

Crunchcrunchcrunch on the pavement. Swishswish-swish through the grassy island. The beep of his truck unlocking. Our hands meeting on the passenger handle as we both went for it. Mine winning. His grin in the rearview mirror as he walked around. And the slamming of doors, sealing us in the small space together and alone.

Shit, Hannah.

I tried to remember I loved my friend more than Sam. I mean, how could I love him? We'd only been in school together for all of time. I only knew everything about him, what with being friends since sixth grade.

Hannah and I went back further, though. We were tied tighter. Glancing out the window into the silent world beyond, I found her arms crossed and her lips in that perfected only-child pout. Opening the door, I got out and let her slide in next to Sam. More distance was easier. Safer. Plus, she lived farther away. It would make sense he'd drop me first.

Sam turned the key and the radio jumped to life. Turning

the volume down, he pulled out of his parking spot and headed toward the street.

"I was at your game the other day," Hannah said, as I watched his hands on the wheel. Boy hands were an interesting thing. Knobby and awkward.

Wait. What? "*We* were at your game the other day," I corrected.

"I noticed," he replied.

"You're amazing to watch," she cooed. "Have I ever told you that?"

He smirked a little into the windshield. "A few times."

"You passed Marin's house," she said, pointing toward my street.

"I figured I'd take you home first since Marin lives closer to me."

That was true. Smart thinking on his part.

"Her mom can get kind of manic, though, if she's late."

Also true. But Sam kept driving.

Hannah and I were only children. We were each other's first line of defense—that's what she'd always told me. I'd needed her way more than she needed me, though, which meant I owed her. So I'd spent a year trying to avoid him. It should be getting easier, not harder.

"Okay, but who really wants to go home?" Hannah asked. "Let's do something fun."

I considered it. "Like what?"

"I have to get to work in a bit," Sam said, glancing at me.

Hannah looked over, like why wasn't he glancing at her?

Because he liked me. Because he'd been sending me texts. Cute ones I hadn't told her about, asking if I was going to be somewhere, telling me it wouldn't be as fun without me. *It's been too many days since we hung out, Marin Greene.*

I tried not to text him back, only caving when he asked me a direct question that would be rude not to answer.

"Oh, come on," Hannah recovered. She always recovered, and quickly. "The weather is perfect for my hot tub. Nice and crisp."

"Jon likes hot tubs," Sam said. "And he doesn't have a job."

"Jonathon Parker is bald," Hannah said. She could go on for hours about this. *Why would a teenager shave his head? Wouldn't there be plenty of time to do that later in life?*

Sam laughed. "Not because he has to be."

She tsked. "Because he's crazy."

"Because the ladies love it."

"Not this lady."

"Why not?"

"I guess because I like someone else." She ran her hand over *his* head like I so wanted to do. I scratched my palm and she added, "Someone who has hair."

"You and Jon would be great together," Sam insisted.

"We would not. Tell him, Marin—Jonathon and I would not be great together."

Actually, I kind of agreed with Sam. "He only shaves his head so the muscles in his neck stand out more."

Sam cracked up at this. But really, Jon was a beast, finely tuned. "Seriously, he told me that once."

Hannah huffed. "His muscles stand out enough on their own."

Sam lifted his sleeve and clenched his bicep. "I've got nothing on Jon."

Crossing her arms, Hannah slumped back against the seat. "You've got plenty on him."

"He has liked you since second grade," I reminded.

"He only likes me at this point because I'm the only girl who doesn't think he's hot shit."

Sam cracked up at that, too. "This is my best friend we're talking about."

"I'd say it to his face."

"And *that's* why he likes you," I pointed out. Sam caught my eye and we grinned.

"Not helping," Hannah muttered, her stare searing the smile right off my face as Sam pulled into her long driveway.

"Really, though, the four of us should go out sometime," Sam said.

Neither of us replied, because that wasn't how it worked. No one took the steering wheel from Hannah and put her in the back seat with a discard. She was the one who filled the seating chart.

I opened the door to let her out, and as I was getting back in, she held her cell up—*text me asap*.

Yes, she'd want every second of our alone time documented, I knew.

Holding mine up—*yes, asap*—I slid back in the truck.

Sam peeled out like we were escaping something, then slowed as he pulled onto the next street. "Jon said you and Hannah did the choreo for the football game last week."

"Yeah. Mostly Hannah."

"Why mostly Hannah?"

"She cares more than I do."

"About dance?"

"About control."

He chuckled.

"I mean, no offense to her—"

"I get it." He glanced over at me and smiled, stopping the truck at the bottom of my mom's driveway.

I hopped out before I could accidentally-on-purpose talk to him for hours until we were accidentally-on-purpose making out. Closing the door with the kind of slam that illustrated how I felt about my choice, I waited for him on the cracked sidewalk. Cracked, but without weeds, sort of like the rest of the neighborhood. The lawns, houses, trees, and bushes had all been around for a while, long enough that they showed their age, but well-kept enough that ugly overgrowth hadn't taken over.

Sam didn't have any weeds, and as far as I could tell, he

didn't have any cracks, either. He not only played soccer but also worked at the grocery store, had one sister, and had lost his dad when he was little. He was always eating vegetables at lunch instead of the good stuff, the stuff with sugar and fat and calories. My mom would approve.

The living room curtains parted, and half her face hung in the shadow. Point three of contention: she needed to get her own life.

"Thanks for the ride," I told him as he came around the truck.

"I have to work tonight," he said. "But maybe we could hang out tomorrow after my game?"

"I can't. Not that I don't want to, but my mom..." I winced in apology. I could already hear her: *Thursday nights are my nights.* It had been a huge battle getting my weekends off for friends—there was no way I could get a Thursday, too. "We're all going to the football game Friday, right?"

"Sure, but I meant—"

"I know." He'd meant just us. But I couldn't do that.

"You like me, Marin Greene, I know you do."

I smirked. "How do you know that?"

"Aside from the heart emojis you're so fond of?"

I scoffed. "Please, I send those to all the boys."

"Then how about"—he paused to lean in—"because I like you so much it doesn't seem possible it could be one-sided." His face was set, serious, stone cut into diamond, and his eyes were a force of whirling severity.

Swallowing that intensity straight to my belly, I held my breath until I was sure the right words would come out, the kind that didn't let on how badly I wanted to throw myself at him. I held my breath until I could inch away from the pull and not melt into a pool of goo at his feet. I held my breath until I could smile haphazardly, like we were just joking around. "It's one-sided for many people, Sam Hanson, or there would be no heartbreaks to write songs about."

"You're not denying it, though?"

"Marin!" my mom called through the screen.

"I have to go."

He looked down at our feet and tapped my toe with his. "You're not denying it."

"I'll see you tomorrow at school, Sam."

He looked up with a frown and my phone buzzed. Hannah, probably.

Right. Hannah.

"Thanks for the ride," I choked out.

Putting his hands deep in his pockets, he nodded as I headed up the driveway. I turned on the front step as he got in his truck and drove off, then told myself once again to forget about him.

The door flung open. "Who was that boy, and where have you been?"

"Mom, don't spy."

"What else can I do? It's not like you keep a diary anymore."

"Because you'd read it."

"Exactly, but then I wouldn't have to spy." I brushed past her and dropped down on the couch, belly first, hoping that this time it would cocoon me, rinse my brain through with bleach, and purge Sam from my bones.

He was laced into my veins, my circulation, every beat of my pulse reminding me of Him Who I Could Not Have.

My mom sat on the couch next to me and put a hand to my forehead. "Are you sick?"

"No."

"Tired?"

"No."

"If you're not tired, why are you lying down?"

"Because sometimes I want this couch to swallow me."

"I know. I need to get a new one." She clasped her hands together in her lap. "He's really no one?"

"Please don't make a big deal out of this. He's just a friend who drove us home."

"Okay. Then let's finish your application for KU."

Burying my face in the soft, worn, yellow fabric, I mumbled. "I told you I don't want to stay in town."

"It doesn't hurt to apply here, Marin. Then if you don't get in anywhere else, you have a backup plan."

"Thanks for the vote of confidence."

"I don't know how it's such an easy decision for you, leaving me for college." Her hands started to twist in her lap. Limp fish gasping for breath.

"Mom."

"Don't 'Mom' me." She sniffed. "You go far away and it's all over."

"Me going far away doesn't mean I won't need you."

"You hardly need me now!" she cried, the change in her tone a dare that I refused to fall for. Instead, I would look at the flat, cheerful buds on the drapes until she calmed down. I would not argue about how I wasn't supposed to need her at seventeen, how I was supposed to be self-sufficient. Not that she'd ever really been a pillar to lean on. More like quicksand. It wouldn't matter anyway if I did say it because she only ever heard herself.

It wasn't worth the energy when the outcome was always the same.

"Hannah wants me to go to K-State." She wanted me to go to KU, too, of course, but I wasn't going to admit that I was even considering it. I wasn't. I couldn't. I focused on the flowers again, telling myself this wasn't a concession of any sort, only a fact.

The air was still, stagnant. No breeze from a window or fan or human movement.

She smoothed her yoga pants, stood to rummage around at her desk, and came back to the couch artificially sweetened. "You could do physical therapy there, too?"

"Yes."

"Well, then let's put that one on your list, okay?"

"Sure, of course." Like it had been my plan the whole time.

Chapter 4

...or studio.

I WAS IN THE health-and-beauty aisle, stocking feminine hygiene amidst a fried-chicken smell wafting from the deli, and Whit wouldn't stop texting me even though she knew I was at work.

"Why do you keep buzzing?" Sam asked, poking his head around the end cap. "I'm doing paper towels over here and I can hear you buzzing."

"Whit won't leave me alone." She was on her fifth first date in the last two weeks, going through men fast enough for the both of us. Ignoring her, I tossed Sam a stray package of maxi-pads someone had stuffed in a hole on the shelf. He was standing in front of their designated spot, but instead of catching them and putting them back, he jumped out of the way in what could only be described as horror.

He put his hands up and shook his head. "I won't touch those things."

"You're scared of the sanitary napkins?"

"I wouldn't say I'm scared." But he'd taken another step

back. I threw another package at him, a different brand this time. He shielded himself. "They're slimy! Stop!"

"They're slimy?" Running my finger along the shiny plastic, I laughed. Then threw another, which he avoided by ducking back into his aisle.

My pocket vibrated again, and I went to turn my phone off, but it was a number I didn't recognize.

>when r u going on break

who is this<
>who do u think

my fairy godmother<
santa claus<
god<
please be god<
>plz tell me when ur going on break
>this message brought to u by sam hanson

I grinned and saved his number to my phone, figuring the time it took would keep him squirming.

howd u get my number<
>the work contact list

Duh. How come I hadn't thought of that? I mean, not that I wanted his number.

>U going on break or not?

right this minute?<
or sometime tonight?<

I was watching the screen, waiting, when a throat cleared at the end of the aisle. Worried it was my boss, I shoved my phone in my pocket and looked up innocently. I *had* been vibrating all night.

But it was Sam. "Are you coming or what?"

I couldn't help myself: "Where ya goin'?"

He shook his head and waited for me to join him, which of course I did. But as we walked through the store, I was careful not to touch him, not to brush arms or lean into him like my body seemed to want.

Sam could be fun if he understood the parameters, but best to make sure those were clear first.

"Break room or out back?" he asked. We'd reached the rear corner of the storage room where we punched in and out. To the right, stairs led down to the horror-movie basement and its drippy, dingy break room. In front of us was the door to the loading dock where the trucks came in.

"Out back."

He pushed the door open and held it for me.

My phone buzzed again, and I retrieved it, told Whit I was on break with Sam Hanson, and put it back in my pocket. That would shut her up, at least for fifteen minutes.

"I have a soccer game tomorrow," he said, pulling a vape out of his pocket and offering it to me. "You should come."

Taking an inhale of pineapple coconut, which was...*awful*, I exhaled and wrinkled my nose. "I'm not much of a joiner."

Sam smiled a little. "You don't have to join. You just have to watch."

Watching him might be fun, but the packed bleachers and obnoxious fans? "I'm not really into organized activities."

"Does that mean you've never been to a football game?"

"Once. Freshman year."

"Really?" He tilted his head. "What do you do with all that extra time?" As if I was some curious specimen who had hours of free time due to my lack of school spirit.

I studied him, in his untucked uniform with his pretty-boy face, and decided he hadn't meant to sound insulting. "I dance."

He shot me a look. "Marin, I know all the girls on the dance team."

I smirked. "I bet you do."

"Not like that!" His cheeks flushed all the way through. "Anyway, it doesn't count if it's just something you do in your room."

A surprised, scoffing laugh fell out of me. "I dance competitively, Sam."

"Please be serious. I want to know what you like to do."

His face was so sincere, almost as if I'd insulted him, that I couldn't help but prove it. Handing the vape back to him, I pushed away from where I'd been settled against the wall. Humming my solo from last year, I sank into the motions immediately. Lifting up, folding over, then up again. Swinging an arm out to the side, and most of my body with it, then the other. Spin, collapse, rolling up off my toes, reaching and reaching and folding and hurting—the song was about being trapped, trying to get out, get free—then spins and jumps and leaps and turns, catching myself at the edge of the dock/stage (on purpose), as the door shot open with a bang. I stumbled to a stop as Kesh joined us.

Like Sam and I, Kesh was a senior, and the three of us made up the West High contingent of Fiesta Grocers. This meant we stuck together at work, even though we didn't run in the same circles at school. Not that I really had a circle.

"Wow." Sam let this word out on a heavy exhale.

The way he looked at me, wide-eyed and dumbstruck, like I'd handed him over a secret or turned myself inside out, like he *knew* things about me he couldn't un-know—well, I couldn't stand there and make normal conversation with the two of them. Cutting my break short, I headed back to work and spent the rest of my shift trying to shake free of it, the feeling that he'd seen straight inside me. That he'd been paying that close attention.

I was punching out when Kesh grabbed my hand and led me through the back door. Sam was waiting for us, leaning against his truck. We all piled in, me squished in the middle, and as Sam turned the keys just enough to start the radio, he offered his vape to me.

I shook my head this time, remembering his poor choice in flavor, and rested back against the seat, singing along with the song spilling out of the speakers. It was about a bird that wouldn't shut up, so the singer splits it in half only to find herself inside.

Kesh unloaded his backpack—calculus and physics and a pile of novels from AP Lit—to retrieve a bottle of flavored vodka, compliments of his older brother, no doubt. "The lady, as always, takes the first sip."

I obliged, then held it out to Sam.

He didn't take it, but said, "You aren't buzzing anymore."

I pulled my phone out of my pocket and turned it back on. Whit was probably going mad about now, what with my cryptic Sam text and no real dirt. The score was best friend: five, Mom: one. My mom didn't usually bother me too much when I was working, but now that my shift was over, she was bound to get started.

Looking back up, I offered the bottle to Sam again. He shook his head. "My little sister will be up when I get home."

I smirked. Of course. Always the good example. I handed it back to Kesh and he nursed it for close to an hour as we talked. At approximately 9:56, I shoved into Sam for him to let me out. He hung a hand on the top of his open door as I scooted across the seat with a goodbye for Kesh, who was gathering his contraband and heading home, too.

As I landed on the pavement, Sam said, "Good night, Marin," but his tone was so thick and deep it felt like he was saying something more.

"'Night, Sam," I whispered, shaking it off and heading over to my car, a few empty spots away.

"You sure you're okay to drive?" he asked. "I'd love to take you home."

I grinned. "You would, would you?"

He flushed, quickly and completely. "Happy to, I mean, if you need a ride."

"I had one sip, Sam. An hour ago." Walking straight at him, heel to toe, with both index fingers on my nose, I smirked before stopping in front of him to bow. "Sober as can be, I promise."

We glanced at Kesh, who was making a lot of noise trying to mount his bike. Taking it from him, I hoisted it into the back of Sam's truck. "Sam's offering up rides tonight, Kesh."

And like the obedient boy he was, Sam slid into his car, buckled Kesh in, and pulled out with a sad smile in my direction.

Life would be easier if he didn't like me. But not as fun. Though, maybe I was misreading him. Maybe Whit didn't know what she was talking about. Either way, he'd surely just complicate my life, which I definitely didn't have time for.

When I got home, my mom was standing in the center of the kitchen, lights off. She was sniffling, and, judging by the pile of tissues on the counter and the puddles at my feet, must have been at a slow weep for a while.

"Where've you been?" She blew her nose. "I called you a million times. Do you have any idea how worried I was?"

"What could you have possibly been worried about? I was at work."

"That you'd end up in a ditch somewhere! That you were on your way home and got in a car accident! That you stopped at a stop sign and someone pulled you out of the car to assault or molest you! There are a million things that could have happened on your way home!"

"In this neighborhood? Really?" I crossed my arms. "Is Dad also worried?"

"Your father is asleep."

I made a face, as if this proved my point.

"You got off work an hour ago. What exactly have you been doing?"

I wanted to tell her I was screwing a stranger in the back of my car while the parking lot watched, but instead, I told her the truth. "We were vaping and drinking in Sam's truck."

She turned for her spot at the counter, designated as

such by the Kleenex debris. "Don't exaggerate just because you think I'm being overprotective," she said. "You know how I feel about lying."

Right. "We were just talking, Mom."

"You wouldn't do this to me if you knew what kind of day I had."

"Whatever, I'm going to bed."

Her pouts were amazing—committed and child-like—but also, on an adult, traitorously disgraceful. "We're supposed to be a team, Marin. My mother and I? She was always there for me."

"The exact comparison there, Mom, would be to note that unlike Gram always being there for you, you are not, in fact, always there for me."

"How can you say that?" She gasped. "I'm your mother. Of course I'm always there for you."

One thing I'd learned, living with my mom, was that a gasp inserted into the middle of a sentence was only a melodramatic play for sympathy. A true gasp of shock must come immediately if it's to be deemed a naturally occurring event.

She worked the pout again. "I want us to be there for each other."

"Fine, Mom." I pulled up a stool. "Let's try this out. I'm here for you."

Her lip trembled as she gazed at me. "I'm just so lonely. And what am I *doing* with my life? Why did I start teaching yoga?"

"Because you were there so often, they figured you might as well be paid."

She frowned.

Running my hands up and down my jeans, I tried again. "Do you think you'd feel more fulfilled if you offered privates?"

"Ugh, you're just like your dad."

"How's that, exactly?"

"Always pushing me. As if forcing me down a path is going to help. I need support, okay?"

"Fine. You have my support in whichever path you want to take forward. My turn now?"

"What do you mean?"

"My turn to share what's bothering me and your turn to show support?"

She heaved out a sigh. "Can't you see that now's not the best time for me?"

"Take it or leave it."

My mom pressed fingertips to her forehead. "Fine."

"Imani said if I want to keep competing with the studio, I need to take some group classes. I'm not the oldest anymore, so even though I'm teaching, all the other kids are wondering why I get special treatment. But I'm afraid if I commit to too much, my grades will slip, and I have to keep them up for college admissions."

I wanted to dance at Chapman in California, which I

might be able to sneak into with a 3.8, but then the problem was how to pay for it. They'd been pretty adamant about making it work financially if they wanted you, but it still meant I couldn't quit my job—or teaching at the studio.

"That doesn't sound very fair of Imani," my mom said. "She can't just be okay with something for three years and then change her mind on you like that."

"She can, though. She owns the place."

"You should write her a letter." My mom straightened in her chair and raised her brow. "Want me to write her a letter?"

"No. I want you to stop making me pay for my car insurance and start giving me gas money." So I could maybe work just a little less.

She frowned. "Absolutely not."

"Mom."

"I said no."

Resting my elbows on the counter, I ran my fingers through my hair and tugged. She. Never. Heard me. And Dad would go for it, he'd say sure, but then she'd be on his case, breathing fire and making him take it back.

That's pretty much what he'd told me when I'd asked him.

"Do what you think is best. Worst case, you end up at KU."

"KU does not have a dance major." And it would mean I'd be within her reach.

"Yes, they do!"

I bit my tongue. I wanted a dance program I had to audition for. If it was pay-for-play, it would be harder to know how it would pan out in the professional sector. I did my best to control my frustrated tears. "And why would you want me to stay here?"

"Why wouldn't I? You're my baby."

"You hate me. Pretty sure you'd be happier if I *didn't* live here."

"Please, Marin. You might frustrate me on a daily basis, but I don't hate you."

"You say mean shit to me all the time."

"And you say mean shit to me," she snapped. "Stop being so childish."

"You *taught* me how to say mean shit to you."

"This is exactly why I need yoga."

I threw my hands up in the air but, for once, remembered myself.

Remember yourself, Marin. Stop crying. Words she'd said but never lived by. *It's worse for me. You'll understand someday.*

Well, I understood now. I understood she made it worse for herself, that she chose it and, for some twisted reason, she liked it that way. I wouldn't let her drag me under, no matter how much I had to fight it. And I wouldn't be sorry for that, either.

I ground my teeth for control while she looked at the

patch of moonlight on the floor, her dark hair falling free of her bun and the smudged makeup on her eyes contributing to the depressing image she was trying to feed me.

"Maybe if you told me you loved me once in a while," she murmured, "the frustration would be worth it."

But see, if you listened instead of looked, you could hear the truth of her. "And now you're saying I'm not worth the frustration I cause you."

She shot a look up at me. "Even when asked, you can't say 'I love you'?"

"I love you, Mom." But I said it to the wall clock because what I really wanted to do was scream.

She pulled me into her without getting up off the stool, her hands on my arms, a hug that was never really a hug. "I love you, too." Pushing back, her eyes narrowed. "But it hardly counts when you have to be asked."

Due to the look on her face, the one that pegged *me* as cruel, I stood. Offering her nothing but a sneer, I replied, "Just like it hardly counts when you can't say it first."

Chapter 5

Either Hannah...

THE SUN WAS SHINING on the empty field beyond the school parking lot. A skinny path had formed inside the seldom-mowed patch of grass, and I sat in it.

When we were in seventh grade, if Hannah had an appointment after school, Whitney and I would stop in this field on our walk home. It was on high school property, and we'd pretend we were older—old enough to belong there—because neither of us wanted to walk into the tension of our respective houses. When Hannah wasn't busy, we could go to her place after school, where tension didn't seem to exist.

It had been the one thing Whitney and I had kept from Hannah—our one secret—because Hannah wouldn't have understood sitting in a field pretending to be something we weren't.

Was I here in this secret place that Hannah had never touched because I wanted to pretend Sam and I could be together?

We'd gone to the football game Friday and out with

friends after. And every day this week, he'd waited for me in the cafeteria until I was done with dance so he could take us home. Each time, he dropped Hannah off first, no matter what kind of spin she put on it.

She hadn't told me I couldn't date him. It was just her face every time he picked me over her. Of course, I could have asked her, but she hadn't brought it up, which was sort of approval in and of itself. We both knew if she wanted—or didn't want—something, she'd make it known.

Though, she'd also had plenty of opportunity to step back in the last week and let it happen, and she hadn't. Instead, she got in Sam's truck every time he offered to drive me home, and after we dropped her off, she'd text me before we could even make it to my driveway, asking if we talked about her, what we talked about, had he tried anything?

Footsteps swished along the dirt path, and I put a hand up to shade my eyes as Sam stopped over me.

"I thought that was you out here." He smiled. "Wishing on dandelions?"

"Wishing I had something to do, maybe." *Or just wishing on you.*

"Wanna come eat with me? I'm going to Big Mike's."

"You're eating dinner right now?" I checked my phone. It was only four o'clock.

"Afternoon snack."

I had a screaming ball of yes building up in my chest,

catching new speed every time I caught a glimpse of him. Sometimes, late at night, when I was alone and not answering his texts, I'd even whimper a bit, to let the pressure out. But he was just a boy and I was just in high school, and truly, relationships couldn't matter this much, right? That's what all the adults said anyway—*you're so young, you don't even know yet.* Maybe my mom was right—maybe every teenage pairing was purely based on hormones. But then, why did my hormones only want him? Why weren't they less selective?

If I took him for mine, it might actually break Hannah and me. She might stop talking to me like she did Whitney freshman year. Or talk to me, but not really pay attention, like she did with everyone else who'd wronged her. Could she overlook it, like when...

Yeah, I couldn't think of a time she'd overlooked anything.

I sighed. "I'm good, thanks."

"You don't have to eat, just keep me company."

"Not today."

"But today's the perfect day." His eyes were soft, and I knew what he meant—perfect because Hannah was not there. I would have thanked her doctor's appointment if I could will myself to take what I wanted.

But then, if I did, and Sam and I were terrible together and fizzled out, she'd still know I'd picked him over her. She'd still feel rejected. By me. The one person she trusted not to reject her.

I shook my head. "I can't."

"You can."

I shook my head again.

"Tell me you don't like me, and I'll leave you alone."

"Of course I like you, Sam. We've been friends forever."

"You know what I mean." He squatted down to my level, his smile forgotten and his face stern. "Until you tell me I don't have a chance, I'm not giving up on us."

With a soft smile, I tilted my head. "We're an 'us' already?"

"Can't you be serious?"

"I'd rather not." *But not for the reasons you think.*

He stood with a sigh. "So you won't come with me?"

"No."

"Never, or just not today?"

I pulled up a handful of grass and threw it at him. "Stop it!"

"Stop tempting you?"

I laughed. "Just go!"

"What are you going to do?"

"Homework."

"Here?"

I nodded, and he sighed. After watching him walk away, I dropped flat to the ground.

I was in too deep. Drowning. But what exactly was suffocating me right now, watching him walk away? What was choking my gut every time he glanced at me or smiled or smirked or gave me those amused, secret looks? And could I get through an entire year of school, put up with him being perfect every day, and manage to keep his lips off mine? Especially if he refused to back off unless I told him he had no chance. Could I even force myself to say that out loud, knowing how it would hurt?

I should care more about hurting Hannah. He would survive.

Not that she wouldn't. She was an only child, used to standing alone, and full of herself enough to be resilient. For all I knew, she'd handle it better than he would.

I rolled on my side. The grass swayed in the light breeze, and my backpack taunted me with all the things I should be more concerned with than stupid boys.

AP Calc might be easy, but Physics was giving me hell. AP Lit might be enjoyable, but AP History? If I had to memorize one more date, so help me...

Caught between lamenting my love life and the homework I didn't want to do was how Sam found me when he came back.

"You're being very productive, I see."

I shot up. How could he have gotten hotter in the twenty minutes it took to run to Big Mike's?

Sitting cross-legged, he set his white paper bag in front of him and dug a cookie out of it. "For you. Double peanut butter deluxe, because it doesn't get better than that."

I agreed. It didn't get better than Sam Hanson.

"Take it," he prompted.

But I wanted to take him.

"Come on, Marin, don't let a good cookie go to waste."

How could I let him go to waste?

"It's not like a promise ring or anything."

With a frown, I snatched the cookie from his hand.

Between bites, we talked about the coming weekend. There was another football game on Friday, and we were learning our competition jazz routine all day Saturday. Sam worked both Saturday and Sunday night, and my mom had asked me to assist a yoga class with her Sunday afternoon—some mother/daughter special she was promoting.

Point four of contention: maybe use me once in a while as an example of how to do a pose right, instead of always how to do a pose wrong.

"What about Sunday morning?" he asked.

"I'll be volunteering."

"Where?"

"At the food pantry off Main."

He crumpled the paper his sandwich had been wrapped in and stuffed it back in the bag. "You go by yourself?"

"Sometimes my mom comes with." Probably only to prove she could be selfless, too.

Point five of contention: if I'm nice to a sweet homeless boy, it doesn't mean I want to jump him, and please don't tell his mother that I do.

Though maybe I should consider it. Would it help me forget about Sam?

"How about that, then?" he asked. "I could come with."

This was when it clicked that he was trying to figure out when we could be alone again, the two of us. Embarrassing really, how long that took. "You'd want to do that?"

"Of course, what heartless soul wouldn't?"

"Um, well, Hannah."

He choked a little, but it was an amused kind of choke.

"She's not a heartless soul," I defended. She was always buying me stuff when she went shopping with her mom, little things that reminded her of me. And she always shared everything—her gum, her lipstick, her snacks, her shoes.

"I didn't say she was," he said.

"You sort of did."

"I'm sorry. It was like a trap I walked into backwards."

"Are you saying I set you a trap?"

"I would never say that."

"But I bet you'd also say that you'd never call my best friend a heartless soul."

"Are you teasing me right now? Or did I piss you off? Because I can't really tell."

"Totally teasing."

This time he let it out, his laugh.

"But no more talking crap about my best friend," I warned.

"Never. I would never knowingly talk crap about your best friend."

"It is like pulling teeth to get her to come, though."

"Heartless soul," he muttered.

Feigning offense, I lightly backhanded him, but my smile won out. He knew better. He knew how generous she was. Catching my fingers in his, he rubbed a rough thumb pad against my palm. I yanked my hand away like it stung.

It did—the fact that I couldn't have them both: the boy I wanted and my best friend.

"I should probably head home," I said, pulling my untouched backpack to me and standing up. "My mom gets cranky if I don't make it for dinner."

"Can I drive you?"

"I don't think that's a good idea." Flinging my bag over my shoulder, I looked in the direction of my mom's. It wasn't far. And I needed to walk him off.

"Marin." He said my name like it could reach out and catch me.

"Thanks for the cookie," I replied, as my goodbye. Then I turned and nearly ran.

A block later, when he was out of sight, I texted Hannah to see what she'd say:

       sam wants to come to the shelter sunday<

>i do too!!!!

                      really?<

> **you never want to come<**
>there aren't usually cute boys there

> **pick you up at 8<**
>you know i don't get up til 10

> **i think sam likes me<**
>he told you?

> **yeah<**
>did you tell him you liked him back

> **not yet<**

As I walked home, a deep hook of angst dug its way through me. The wanting to smooth things over with her, the needing things to be right with us, the disruption of our normal—all of that tugged and yanked at me, suffocating everything else. Overriding everything else. How could I betray her by taking what she wanted? Even if she'd never had it. We were tight. Inseparable. That's what was important.

Heading up the driveway, I added, **i won't do anything about it if you don't want me to**, and after slipping my phone in my pocket, I opened the front door.

My mom was sitting on the couch with a book. Setting it aside, she eyed me. "Don't you look all hot and bothered."

I paused before stepping in. How could she know me so little and yet pin that tail on the donkey? "I'm not."

"You look it. What were you doing?"

"Homework."

"Homework *would* make you all hot and bothered."

"What's that supposed to mean?"

"You're kind of a goody-goody."

"Mom!"

"What? There's nothing wrong with that."

"I'm going upstairs," I decided. But once in my bedroom, with the sterile queen bed that took up most of the space, I regretted it.

It was an echo of my real life—a weak, secondhand version. Everything in the closet would have been donated a long time ago if I didn't have two houses, and the walls were colorless and cold. Why decorate when it was only a place to sleep if you couldn't be in your own bed? Like a hotel. An endless string of nights in a hotel. I was a cheap, traveling saleswoman.

Sinking to the floor, I figured I should get going on the homework I'd told my mom I'd already done. But only ten minutes in, she was yelling up the stairs that dinner was ready.

As I sat down at the table, she picked up her knife, then set it down. Grabbed her napkin and unfolded it in her lap. Reached for her fork but let her fingers rest on it instead of picking it up. She took a drink of ice water. Lots of ice. Because then your body had to work harder to warm it to 98.6 degrees.

"Was it a boy?" she asked.

"What?"

"I realized maybe it was a boy."

"No, it wasn't a boy."

"I just thought maybe you needed the privacy of your room to, you know…"

"Mom." I put my hands over my ears.

"This is important stuff, Marin. You need to know you can say no or have the tools to protect yourself if you decide to say yes. You are the only person in charge of your body. Boys don't always get that, so you need to. You need to really feel it, to know what you want is not something to apologize for, even and especially if what you want is to say no."

"Sam is so not like that!" I cried. And inside that murky quicksand where who I hoped he was got twisted with who my mom assumed him to be, it took a while for her smirk to register. She'd gotten it out of me.

Erg.

Stepping over that land mine with a snort, she replied, "You probably think your dad isn't like that, either."

Point six of contention: differing world views. I didn't think it was so awful to have a more positive outlook on men and my own willpower than she did. Also, my dad? Must she bring him into it? Gross.

"So, you have a boyfriend." She swallowed and bit down on her lower lip. "This is the guy from the other day? Why didn't you tell me when I asked?"

Point seven of contention: there was no halfway with

her—once I started, she wouldn't let me stop. I couldn't *choose* what bits of myself to hand over, couldn't protect any of my insides. Once I handed her the end of the rope, she would pull and pull and pull until she had it all. Then she would tell her fifteen closest friends and yoga acquaintances where and when and how. They would pick it apart, laugh at the mistakes I made, and she would come back at me with their suggestions.

Point eight of contention: even though she had no boundaries, I was not an open book.

"I told my mom everything. She was my rock. And you never..." Drip, sniffle, snort. "I can feel it already, that I'm losing you, aren't I? Come college, I'm going to lose you." Her voice trailed off and she pinched the bridge of her nose tight.

Point nine of contention: her emotional mess should not be my problem, but she made damn well sure it was.

So, for the sake of my sanity and this conversation, I agreed. Yes, Mom. Okay, Mom. Whatever you say, Mom. *Let me tell you about Sam.*

Chapter 6

...or Whitney.

I DROPPED MY BAG down by my favorite tree, even though the overweight blossoms were long gone and the branches nearly empty of leaves. This particular magnolia separated the high school from the elementary school playground, which was usually vacant after classes let out. Sometimes there was a stray mother and child, but for the most part, it was all mine.

I'd been hiding here a lot lately, since Whit was busy with her newest boyfriend. She liked making out more than I did, and I liked being alone more than she did, so we were a pretty perfect pair. Unzipping my backpack, I felt for my phone when a shoe appeared at the corner of my vision.

Sam's shoe.

His hand curled around a branch above him, and a wide smile splayed across his face like he'd caught me in another secret.

Not that dancing was my secret. It wasn't. Anyone who frequented a studio in town had seen me around.

"Watcha doin'?" he asked, dropping cross-legged before

I could decide if I wanted him to join me or not.

"I need to pick the songs for my solos," I replied, not pointedly. If I wanted him to leave, I'd say it.

"Solos, plural?"

"Just two."

"Can I hear?"

I sighed, uncertain I wanted to welcome him into more of my world like that. Except, I could use the help. "Only if you vote."

"Really?" Like it was a gift.

"No, never mind." I popped an earbud in my ear, and he snatched the other one out of my hand. I leveled a warning look at him. "This is important, Sam. I need you to be all business."

He smirked a stupid grin, if that was even possible. "I promise."

I reached into my bag for a notebook, ripped a piece of paper out, tore it in four pieces, and handed him two of them. Also, we needed pens.

Five songs later, he wasted no time scribbling. I, however, fell back to the side of the trunk and lay in the grass, my cheek pressed against the blades. I loved all the options and could see each one in chunks and pieces. The question was, what did I feel like dancing out?

Anguish? Always a favorite.

Power? Easy choice, though not as emotive. I was an emotive dancer—ironic, since I was so not emotional in the rest of my life.

Love? Not usually, but this song...

Hope? Obviously last on my list, but I could not get over the beat and the things I could do with it.

Or, finally, creepy. That one probably wouldn't win anything, but it would be amazing.

"Your hat is waiting," Sam said, jiggling his papers between his hands.

Choosing anguish and creepy, I dropped the folded papers into his cupped palms. He shook them like they were dice, then moved his thumb aside just enough to let me reach inside.

"Drumroll, please," I requested.

He thrummed it in his throat somehow, and I raised an eyebrow.

"Very impressive." Unfolding the paper, I announced, "Creepy!"

He groaned.

"What? You didn't like that one?"

"Of course I didn't. *Who* would like that one?"

"Okay, but..." I forced out an exhale, hopped to my feet, stuck an earbud back in his ear, and pressed play.

I'd already imagined the first three eight-counts. It was pretty vigorous, and maybe it wouldn't win, but by the look on his face, it would pull applause. Lots of it.

Panting with exertion, I ended with my hands on my hips. "See?"

"What was that? Lyrical?"

I raised my brow. "Have you been researching dance styles, Sam Hanson?"

"I was trying to figure out what you were doing that night at work. It didn't look like ballet."

I nodded. It had been a lyrical piece. "And this would be contemporary."

"It was...amazing."

"You approve, then."

"Of how you move, not the song."

Letting my shoulders drop and my hands hang at my side, I crashed back down next to him. "Okay," I motioned my fingers, grabby and impatient. "Hands, please."

He shook the remaining papers and held them up above my head this time, like I'd rigged the last one. I gave him a look. He shrugged. "No cheating."

"Anguish!" I shot a hand up in the air, triumphant. Then dropped it. "Wait, I got both of mine?"

He shrugged one shoulder.

"What'd you pick?" But he was making a fist. "Honestly, Sam, I want to know."

"Why? What would you do with that knowledge?"

"Nothing, I just want to know."

"It doesn't matter, then."

I reached for his hand but before I could grab it, he had his arm stretched in the other direction.

I whimpered, more for fun than for real, but it worked.

The noise was barely out of my mouth and his hand was open in my lap, the papers there for the taking. His face hardened into something serious and breathtaking, like I was taking his breath—me, because that's where his focus was, which only made me feel terrible, like I'd been playing with him, giving him ideas.

"Sam…" I warned. Because what more could I say? Nothing felt like it made sense to say out loud. Everything felt like it was happening in undertones.

I shook my head and opened his choices: anguish and hope.

"Show me hope?" he asked softly, the words a higher tone than normal. A plea? Which matched what I had in mind for the song, so okay. I stood, not bothering to turn the music on, and went off what was in my head.

Caught up, I kept improvising, and as my last move, I landed on the ground, head bent in submission.

"I have never enjoyed silence quite so much," he muttered.

"It is nice," I agreed, straightening up.

He raised an eyebrow at me. "Are we both talking about your dancing?"

"No." *Because I don't speak in undertones, Sam.* "I'm talking about silence."

"Oh, I hate silence. Except this way…with you… Do you know how much you just said with your body? The emotion, I felt it." And he went so far as to pound his chest.

"Oh goodness, shut up!" With a laugh, I crawled back over next to him, this time not as close.

"It's true," he muttered.

"What's so bad about silence?" I wondered.

"I'd rather be in someone else's head than my own."

I raised an eyebrow at him. "Is something wrong with your head?"

"No, I just know what's in it already."

"Huh." I nodded. "Good answer." Such a good answer, I had to begrudgingly offer him some points.

"You actually enjoy silence?" he asked. "I mean, really-really, or you were just saying that for the sake of talking?"

"I do not say anything just for the sake of talking."

"Okay, what do you like about it, then?"

The question seemed innocent enough, but the way he was watching me was unsettling, like he was asking why I was the way I was. That look from the other night when I'd danced for him the first time, like he could snake his vision deep into my core and come out with something no one else had yet found.

I closed my eyes to get away from him, to find the silence, the *lack of*. "Silence is peace," I said, opening my eyes. "Freedom. No strings attached. No demands. No need."

He didn't say anything, but insects poured out of his gaze—watching, probing, crawling. A million little eyeballs with legs, scrambling over me, through me, into me.

"That's pretty deep," he finally said.

I shuddered, scratching at my neck. "Don't look at me like that, then."

"Like what?"

"Like you want more."

He let out an amused rush of air and looked down at his hands, which were fiddling with the blades of grass. "But see, I *do* want more."

Our gazes got caught and tangled together. I didn't pull back when he moved forward, but he was doing it so slowly, in such little pieces, that I started to think about how stupid this could get—how bad if he didn't agree to the terms, if he didn't agree to me. But also, I didn't want to hurt his soft, squishy feelings or maybe he wouldn't be so open and vulnerable the next time, and then how would I feel? If he were hard and closed? Part of what I liked so much about him was that he wasn't me.

"Marin!" Whitney's voice broke the moment, just in time.

I cleared my throat and threw an arm up between us to wave at her.

She veered off the sidewalk, pausing with a slight head tilt toward Sam. "I can, um, talk to you later, though."

"No, it's okay. He was just going."

"I was?"

"You were."

He frowned and stood. "When do you work next?"

"Friday night and Sunday. You?"

"What time?"

I squinted up at him. "I don't remember."

He stared at me for a moment as if he was trying to figure me out. I wasn't trying to be mysterious, though; I was just trying not to want him.

"Bye, Sam," I told him.

"Bye, Marin." Then, to her, "Hey, Whitney."

We watched him walk away. Once he'd reached the high school parking lot and was out of earshot, she sank down in front of me.

"What's up?" I asked.

"What do you wear to a symphony?"

I stared at her. "What?"

"A symphony. You know, fancy orchestra music?"

"A gown? Why, your mom trying to wear her littlest black dress to the symphony?"

Whit looked down at her foot and pulled at the laces of her shoe. "You don't think any of her littlest black dresses would work?"

"Sure, she can wear whatever she wants."

"What if it's me wearing it?"

"You're going to a symphony?" I laughed. But she kept picking at her laces and looking at the ground. "Your dad's taking you to the symphony? He must feel really bad about this license thing."

She blew a strand of hair out of her face. "It's a second

date. And my mom doesn't own any gowns."

I blinked at her. She still wouldn't meet my eyes. The kind of guy to spring for tickets to a symphony likely had a car and, even more likely, wasn't our age. Definitely out of high school, and I was going to guess also graduated from college. "Whiiiit," I warned, a slight uptick at the end of her name.

"Your mom doesn't own a gown, does she?"

I frowned. "Whitney, please, you have got to be kidding me."

"I bet Hannah's mom has a gown. Too bad she hates us now."

"How old is this guy?"

She shrugged. "Not that old."

"If you don't tell me, I'm going with fifty, because who the hell goes to the symphony?"

Now she looked at me, but not because she was worried about how I was taking it anymore. Poorly—that's how I was taking it. No, now she was pissed. Good. She should be. If I had to make her pick between me and him, I would. Shooting her chin up a tad, she challenged me. "He's sensitive."

I snorted. "Sensitive until he gets in your pants."

"There are decent men in this world, Marin, whether you and your mom believe it or not."

I narrowed my eyes. She knew better than to bring my mom into this. "My dad is a decent man. You want to date my dad?"

"And here I was going to apologize for running Sam off, but good thing I did, since he's such a shit like the rest of them."

"Of course he's not a shit," I snapped, before I knew what I was saying. Ugh, but Sam was clearly good, through and through. And yes, I imagined even at thirty, he'd be decent enough. Except, "Decent thirty-year-olds wouldn't date a high schooler. Please don't do this."

"How about *you* don't do this. Or I'm going to have to spend the night at my house, when I really need to spend the night at yours."

Taking a deep breath in, I closed my eyes and tried to let it go. It was a second date. No doubt there wouldn't be a third when Whit fell asleep at the symphony. And if her parents were fighting the kind of fight that drove Whit to ask herself over, then that was the bigger problem at hand. Where my mom would at least keep it reasonably together for company, such could not be said for Whit's parents.

"Miri texted me I should avoid going home at all costs. She's already at her boyfriend's."

With a sigh, I wrapped my arms around her. "We can check my mom's closet for a gown."

She kissed my cheek, then wiggled out of my embrace to gather the scattered scraps of paper Sam and I had scribbled on. "Were you guys writing love notes?"

"Picking songs for my solos."

"Shoot! I missed it?"

"I'll play them for you on the way home."

She hopped to her feet and handed me the scraps. "You still have my emergency kit in your glove compartment?"

"Pretty sure you took it for Kyle's."

"Okay, so a drugstore run, too?"

"For candy and a toothbrush?"

"Exactly."

Three songs later, I was trying to best Hannah's ghost at making an ice cream cone while Whitney had one hand on a toothbrush and five tentacles on her favorite sweets.

Of course, to shame me so good, Hannah herself walked in as I was finishing up.

"That hardly hits my baseline," she scoffed, brushing past me. "Barely three inches, I'd say."

"Maybe that's all I wanted," I called after her.

Whit stuck her head out the candy aisle. I nodded toward Hannah at the counter, whispering to Ernie. The rest of Whitney's body emerged, and she sashayed right up next to Hannah like they were still best friends and Hannah wouldn't mind spilling her medical secrets.

Preemptively grabbing a lolly, Whit ripped the wrapper open with her teeth and leaned across the counter over her pile of candy. Ernie held a finger up, then slid into his back shelves where he stored the prescriptions. It was good to know Hannah still kept him in business like Whit and I did.

Ernie came back from his vaults and hobbled over to the cash register. For this reason alone, Whitney and Hannah pasted smiles on their faces. I was still a good bit away.

"It's been a while since you three came in here together," Ernie said, opening his palm for Hannah's change to drip into her own. It was a talent he had, or maybe just the magic of the store, how coins fell at a slower-than-average pace here.

"A lifetime." Hannah said. "And yet, not long enough." Whipping her hair out and causing a tsunami, she fled from the scene in true form—the last person to stick around for a relief effort.

"She hasn't been the same since you all broke up," Ernie muttered.

"She was always a bad egg," Whitney said, sliding her cash across the counter. "Did you know she doesn't like lemon drops?"

Ernie whistled. "That's the true sign of a rotten soul."

Turning with my cone, which Whit was motioning for him to put on her tab, I hurried out to the street, a new secret staked to the spiked collar around my neck.

(I also was not a fan of lemon drops).

Chapter 7

Either yes...

WE PERFORMED AT HALFTIME, then I slipped into the school to change. Most of the team, including Hannah, stayed in dance-team gear throughout the game, but I was too conditioned from the old competition scene to wander around in a costume after any performance.

As I swung out of the locker room, Sam was waiting for me. A large grin bloomed on his face, and his arm shot out to reveal a fat bunch of yellow tulips that hung in the space between us.

"These are for you," he said.

I couldn't help inhaling them. "They're beautiful, Sam."

"I didn't want to do roses—I mean, I would've, but they just seem so overdone. Do you like tulips?"

I nodded. I did. They were my favorite. Well, after sunflowers. But now they might have edged into the first spot. He also handed me a fancy piece of paper. Gilded and sparkling, it was about half the size of a full sheet.

Printed in a loopy script nearly impossible to read, it was fill-in-the-blank:

I accept/don't accept this __________ invitation to the homecoming dance, to which I will be wearing a __________ dress and for which I will expect a __________ corsage. My other favorite colors are ______________, and my favorite food/restaurant is ____________. I hope that night for ______________ and most definitely don't want ______________. You would make my night if ______________ and possibly my year if ______________.

I bit my lip to contain my smile as I finished reading it. "Very cute, Sam."

"I was hoping it might convince you to say yes."

I looked at my fingers, the ones that held the invitation in my hand, the same ones that had texted Hannah—*not yet, no*—and still hadn't heard a response. I mean, she'd called me later to talk about her doctor's appointment and all the tests they'd done but hadn't brought up Sam. She-who-always-had-something-to-say had nothing to say. All I could figure that meant, after poring over the possibilities for three days, was that she couldn't force herself to allow it, but she couldn't force herself to forbid it, either.

Not all that unlike what I did last year when she was actively trying to make him and her happen. Which meant, judging by how I'd felt then, that she didn't like it and I didn't really have her permission.

Ugh, when had my stomach started hurting?

Shaking my head, I pushed all of it back to him—the flowers, the invitation, the implication. "I can't, Sam."

He put his hands behind his back, refusing to take any of it. "Please, Marin. Think about it. I'm not going to ask anyone else."

I dropped the flowers to my side. "I can't."

"You won't, you mean."

"That's not true, I—"

"Has she said: *you can't go out with him*?"

"What?"

"I know this is about Hannah, but she can't chase me forever."

"And you can't chase me forever." It was what I was counting on—to get me out of this—since I was no longer sure I could keep away from him on my own.

"I can. I'm very persistent."

I relaxed onto my heel with a small smile. This—that he wasn't me and that he didn't know how to fold—"It's one of the reasons I like you," I admitted.

He smirked. "You like me, do you?"

I rolled my eyes, and he took a small step forward.

"I mean, I can tell, it's just you're so evasive sometimes, it makes a guy wonder."

"I'm not evasive. I'm not evading."

Another step. "But you keep saying no."

I shook my head, then nodded, then shook my head—no, nodded. I did—I did keep saying no.

Another step. Almost close enough to kiss me. So close I could smell his shampoo, along with the smell of a freshly cut lawn. He smelled like grass and rain and lilac shampoo. He smelled like outside, like boy, like my own personal formula of distilled yearning, and I wanted to bury my nose in his neck.

"You made that quad look easy, Marin," Whitney said, startling us. "You looked great, really." I wanted to scream, but I should be thanking her, a ghost from the past reminding me how fickle best friends could be—how fickle Hannah could be.

Her shirt was half-unbuttoned and the hand on her waist was attached to the slimiest of guys. I wasn't sure where she'd come from but was pretty sure she'd been doing a little of what I wanted to be doing, and then a whole lot more.

"Thanks." It meant more coming from her—from someone I knew wouldn't dole out a compliment lightly, and from someone who probably didn't even like me much anymore.

"If you guys are looking for somewhere to, well, you know, the bathroom down by the science lab is usually empty during these things." Monotone, eyes on the floor, fingers sliding through the bleached stalks of her hair.

"Oh, we're not..." I looked back and forth between her and Sam a few times, then hid the flowers behind my back like she might tell on me. Not that she'd ever have told on me. And she'd definitely never narc me out to Hannah.

This shell of the girl I used to know shrugged as her boyfriend started moving, jerking her away from us. "Later, then."

I wanted to wrap my arms around her and keep her here with me instead of letting her go with him, a boy who would let her walk out of a bathroom unbuttoned and then stand here looking around absently as if Sam and I didn't exist. For all the plans we'd made when we were younger, Whitney seemed tragically off-road. I mean, she was the one who wasn't going to let men define her life. Though, she did have a nice sashay that was kind of entrancing. Was that a product of having sex?

As they swung around the corner, I said, "She was our best friend once."

"Is that why we got the good tip on the bathroom?"

"Good to know to avoid it, if that's what you mean."

He smirked. "Afraid of walking in on something?"

"No, I just wouldn't be caught dead making out in a nasty high school bathroom."

"What you're saying then, is that the probability of us ending up together is higher than you setting foot in that bathroom?"

I gave him a look.

He laughed and offered his arm. I didn't take it but did step up next to him as we headed out of the school.

"Tell me what it will take to convince you," he said.

"An alternate universe." One where Hannah and Jon were happily engaged, and no amount of guilt could be leveraged against me.

"There has to be something."

"A different dimension." One where Whitney was my best friend, and I didn't care what Hannah thought.

"What if Jon asked Hannah and the four of us went together?"

"That would be like rubbing her nose in it." And again, she didn't let go of the steering wheel without a fight. But I was starting to think that Sam might match her stubbornness and not see that as a roadblock.

He stopped and lowered his voice. "Don't you think our drives home after school are rubbing her nose in it?"

I bit my lip. "No more drives home after school."

The back of his hand brushed the back of mine, and when I didn't pull away, he reached a pinky out, looping it around mine. When I still didn't pull away, he grinned at the floor and took my entire hand in his.

"Why are you trying so hard?" I asked, as we started walking again.

"Nothing worth having is easy," he replied. "Hanging out with a girl I don't like is not nearly as much fun as hanging out with a girl I do like, even if she doesn't like me back."

I rolled my eyes. "She does like you back."

He beamed at that. "But she still won't go to the dance with me."

Our footsteps echoed to the beat of my heart. This is something I wanted. Surely, if Hannah loved me like she said she did, she would want me to be happy, to take one thing for myself. When had I last taken anything for myself? Yet, if the roles were reversed, I'd be desperate for them not to get together. I'd be desperate for him, and if she went for it anyway, I'd feel like I meant nothing to her.

She meant something to me.

But so did he. More and more, too. He'd always been one of our friends, but now he felt like *my* friend, my own. We smiled together, only the two of us, and he was always asking what I wanted. *What would you do tonight if you could do anything you wanted? What would you do on vacation if you could do anything you wanted? What would you say to our pompous history teacher if you could say anything you wanted?*

How would I answer Sam right now if I could answer any way I wanted?

"She will," I finally replied. "She'll go to the dance with you."

Shooting a look over at me, Sam tilted his head. "I'm sorry. I must have misunderstood her."

I grinned. "I'll go to the dance with you." It was one dance. People went as friends all the time. It didn't have to mean anything more than a date for the dance, or friends teaming up as a unit for one night. And if more came from it, that was something I'd worry about later.

"See? Trying so hard is working out for me."

I laughed as Hannah appeared in front of us, at the end of the hall we were walking down. She looked at me. At the flowers. At Sam. At our hands that I'd allowed to stay linked, and our smiles, now fading on our faces. Her eyebrows furrowed and she curled her shoulders in like she did when she was having a panic attack.

My first instinct was to throw the tulips in the trash and rush to her, tell her it was a mistake, that there was nothing between Sam and me, that he didn't like me at all—he liked her. But she couldn't control him or who he liked. She could only control me.

A cold, creeping anger settled in then, that of course she'd ruin it, when I finally took what I wanted. As if she was using her panic attacks to control the situation. Which of course she wasn't—I was clearly a total shit for even thinking it—but her mom had wanted to know what preceded them. Well, she might not be paying much attention, but so far it seemed to me that hearing things she didn't like and seeing things she couldn't face were what preceded it. She was a spoiled, rotten—

And then she went down, flat on the floor.

I bolted for her, sliding onto my knees, shaking her. "Hannah! Hannah, look at me!"

But she couldn't. She curled up on her side, seemingly frozen.

"Can you breathe?"

With a shaking hand, she grabbed for mine and set it to her chest. Her heart was pounding like crazy, like it was rocking, trying to get out of her chest. Was this what a panic attack was? I'd spent a lot of time reading about them and knew they could cause an irregular heartbeat, but this was insane, how rapid it was, like the frantic beat of hummingbird wings, if hummingbird wings were made of iron.

"Call 911," I told Sam, the cold anger that had filled me bottoming out to horror. "Call 911!"

Sam sat next to me in the waiting room. I wouldn't hold his hand. Still, I was glad he was there. Hannah's parents were in with her, and the doctor had said it was her heart. All along it had been her heart, not panic attacks.

It was after visiting hours, so they weren't sure I'd be able to go in, but I was staying here until they told me I absolutely couldn't. The last thing she saw couldn't be me, betraying her.

I folded over in my seat. Sam set a hand on my back, and

when I didn't shrug him off, he started running soft circles with his palm. I closed my eyes and willed my tears to stay inside.

I needed to tell him the dance was off. We'd be going with our big group of friends anyway and clearly this was a bad idea. Yet I couldn't form the words, told myself now didn't have to be the time. I could deal with it later when my best friend wasn't struggling with a weak heart. When she hadn't been rushed to the hospital in an ambulance and admitted for observation, let alone who knows what else they'd done to her since she'd gotten here.

"Marin?"

I looked up. Hannah's mom was holding the door to the hallway open with one hand.

"I talked them into giving you five minutes. We're going to try to find something for her to eat."

Shooting to my feet, I glanced back at Sam.

"Only you," her mom said.

He nodded. "I'll wait."

Following Mrs. Watson down the bright hallway, my stomach ached with worry and apprehension. We turned a corner in front of the nurse's station, and then she motioned toward a room. As I walked in, her dad nodded at me and slipped out.

Hannah was hooked up to all sorts of leads and had a white thing on her finger. She wore a hospital gown and was sitting up in the bed, knees bent under a pile of white blankets. Her fingers were in her hair, detangling her curls more urgently than normal.

"How are you feeling?" I asked.

Her fingers slowed, then dropped to her lap with a sigh. "Exhausted. Like I just ran a marathon and almost lost my life to it."

I sank down into the chair next to the bed. "Nothing happened with Sam. I'd tell you if something happened."

She stared at me. "You two are pretty cute together."

"You and I are cute together."

Her cheek twitched, but she held her pout. "We are."

"Your heart, then?"

She nodded. "Not panic attacks at all, come to find out, but an extra pathway in my heart."

"What do they do for that?"

"Oh, you know, just a little heart surgery."

"A little heart surgery," I echoed. A little. I nearly snorted. There could be no such thing. "Hannah."

Shit. *Shit.*

I threw my arms around her and buried my nose in her hair, letting the scent of coconut wrap itself around me. She folded her hands around my arm, where it rested in front of her, and clung to me like she was more scared than she let on.

As I pulled away, she reached around my neck to unclasp the tiny cross from my First Communion that I hardly ever took off. She knew this, and she knew why. My parents had still been married back then, and the night I got it was the last celebratory family dinner I could remember actually feeling celebratory.

If she needed a cross around her neck...if she was grasping for something she normally didn't give a second thought... "The necklace is for your surgery? Hannah, you don't believe in God."

"But I believe in you," she said, swallowing hard. "This necklace is so I have you with me."

"When is it? Tonight?"

"It's not an emergency. They have to schedule it. I don't know yet."

"And until then?"

"There are some nasty drugs to try and keep it under control."

"To try?" I squeaked, letting go of her and sitting back in the seat.

She shrugged. "Let's plan something big for the dance. With the whole group. Something spectacular. To keep my mind off this."

Chapter 8

...or no.

As Whitney and I reached the lot, after a little home-work on our park bench, a pretty sweet car was idling next to mine. Whit skipped forward, not a bit surprised, and tossed herself into the man stepping out before he was even fully standing.

Crossing my arms while they whispered to each other, I waited at my hood for her to introduce us. She hadn't told me she was doing this, throwing us together. If she wanted me to be nice, she should've warned me.

Although maybe she hadn't wanted me to be nice—maybe some small part of her knew this was the stupidest thing she'd ever done.

They were holding hands and emerging from between our cars. "Marin, this is Vic. Vic, Marin."

Vic stuck his hand out at me, but I stared at it until he dropped it back to his side.

I couldn't help it; I was squinting at him. *Where had I seen him before?*

"Need a hint?" he asked, voice rich with honey and

accent, smile lopsided and cut with a scar. "I'm the type not to shit at mile twenty."

My jaw dropped.

This was what I'd used on the hot runner. The one who whistled at us now before we could catcall him. Whit always said she'd screw him in a bathroom with an audience, but she'd been kidding, right? When I said that kind of stuff to my mom, I was always kidding.

Only she was acting like Hannah right now, nearly batting her eyelashes and giggling like an idiot. The giggle sounded like a crow in her throat. *Because she couldn't giggle.* She was Whitney. Whitney didn't giggle.

Her palm slid up Vic's very foreboding arm. "I was alone at the park and Vic stopped to keep me company."

"I sure did," he said, wrapping an arm around her waist and planting a tongue between her lips like they'd been together long enough to get their tongues acquainted.

"Whoa, whoa, whoa, whoa, whoa." Stalking over, I grabbed her hand and yanked her a few feet away. "What is this?"

"I wanted him to meet you," she whispered. "What's your problem?"

"He's a brute. And he could be your father!" I hissed.

"He's hot. And twenty-five. Some men have early hair loss."

"That's not loss, that's bald."

She put her hands on her hips. "Because he shaves it.

Because it's receding."

To this, I simply laughed.

"Thanks a lot, Marin, for being so supportive." Spinning, her hair hit me like jagged knives across my nose. "Come on," she muttered to Vic. "Let's go."

What the hell was happening? Whit went for tall, spindly guys who couldn't throw a baseball, let alone a bat. This douche left his polo unbuttoned all the way to show how much testosterone he had to have in order to build such a thick garden of chest hair.

Whit got in his car and slammed the door, and just like that, they were gone.

I wanted to stagger back to our bench, but I had to get to dance. Thank goodness at least it was dance, because at work this would be spinning in my head until I was dizzy. Dance, at least, would void everything else out.

I'd almost forgotten all about it by the time class was over, and then I stayed to practice my solos. The choreo was complete, but I was still perfecting a few moves that I wanted down by the end of the month. That way, by the start of competition season, my performance would be an inevitable extension of my soul. All the bits worked out until I couldn't not do it right.

I almost lost it on my aerial, though, when I saw Sam's face in the window.

He was relaxed, arms crossed and a loose smile on his face, which was more than I could say for my mom, who happened to be standing next to him. Nothing loose about her—tight pony, tight scowl, tight button-down shirt.

When had she shown up? Whatever, it was good practice. Sometimes, something would throw you off on stage, and you just had to keep going. Ignore it.

Sam was hard to ignore, though. A needle at the edge of my vision, looming larger the longer I knew he was there. Calypso, collapse-o, head to the floor, end music.

Heaving, I pulled myself up and pushed my way out of the room, into the hall.

"What are you doing here?" I asked, unsure exactly who I was speaking to.

Sam filled a cup of water from the cooler in the lobby and held it out for me, but I didn't take it.

"That turn looked a little shaky," my mom said.

The weak turn had come shortly after the aerial, when Sam's face was expanding in my peripheral, like a kid with his nose pressed against the glass of a dollhouse. Me, the doll inside; him, the huge, enraptured innocent.

I'd never loved her for her critiques. "Mom, why are you here?"

Sam startled and turned to her, wiping his hands on his pants before offering her one. "Mrs. Greene! So nice to meet you. I'm Sam. Sam Hanson."

She surveyed him from toes to head: dusty, checkered slip-ons, fresh jeans, fancy navy pullover zipped down to reveal the top of a casual plaid oxford shirt.

Turning back to me, my mom said, "I wanted to see how it was coming."

"You weren't invited."

She jerked her head in Sam's direction. "You let him distract you, but I can't come watch?"

"He wasn't invited, either."

"I, um, I just showed up," he said apologetically to my mom. "I thought it looked great, for what it's worth."

Her smile was tight, but not tight enough that he'd pick up on it. "That's nice, dear, but she is better than what you just saw in there."

Taking the water from his hand, I chugged it, then turned my back on both of them and went to practice my other solo.

I couldn't concentrate, though, because they were talking. He warmed her up, a burning coal in a brick oven, and she was laughing.

Laughing?

When had I last heard her laugh? I loved my mom for her laugh. It was this bright, tinny sound that sent joy up your neck and to your cheeks until you were laughing, too.

Focus, Marin.

Dance was my escape, and from that, I could not be distracted. I aimed to forget and leave it in the mirror, draped on the girl in the reflection.

By the time I was done, six run-throughs and twenty minutes later, it was only Sam still watching.

Normally, I'd stretch hard for at least fifteen minutes while my muscles were warm, but since Sam was there, I unplugged my phone, flipped off the lights, and grabbed my sweater, pulling it on over my leo and tights. I was dripping. Disgusting. Sweat and shed emotions running in rivulets down my torso, front and back.

He'd never want me now.

Only, the way he was looking at me as I walked out, he still did. "You are incredible, Marin. That day at work, I thought—and then, at the park, I mean—but now, this, the whole deal, it's—"

"It's not the whole deal, Sam, until I'm on stage with costume, makeup, and hair. And stop gushing." I brushed past him, grabbed my bag, and headed for the front of the building. "How'd you find me?"

"Hannah."

I stopped and he ran into me from behind, his hands out to catch my arms and steady me. I jerked away. I didn't need steadying. I was perfectly steady alone—that was the whole point.

Turning, I double-checked, "Hannah?"

"She was going on and on about how awesome a dancer she was—"

I laughed. She'd quit the studio when she could no longer place above me.

"—and I asked her where she used to dance, where she learned it all."

I grinned. "You're a sneaky one, Sam Hanson."

"Good. I was afraid you'd think I was stalking you. Sneaky, I can live with."

"I'm sure Hannah would've thought it romantic."

"You don't?"

"What about this has been romantic?"

His face fell.

"Don't worry, Sam. I don't appreciate romance, anyway." Spinning on my heels, I marched to the office to tell Imani I was done and thank her for staying—though I knew it was work she'd be doing here or at home regardless. Down the hall, through the lobby, out into the November chill of the parking lot.

This moment. The jellied exhaustion in my limbs meeting the dusk of night, the sweet smell of dew on its way in, the hush of a suburb gone home after work.

I loomed large in these moments. Powerful. Vital. Strong. Feeling like I could do anything. On my own. Alone.

But there was Sam, right behind me. Not letting me be.

"So, what's up?" I asked, unlocking my car and tossing my stuff inside.

He put up a finger and rushed over to his truck, a few empty spots away. I did my best to wipe the sweat off my face with the bottom of my sweatshirt, and when I dropped it, a massive bouquet of yellow tulips greeted me.

He cleared his throat. "Will you go to Homecoming with

me?"

I balled the sweat-soaked section of my shirt into my fist as I digested the question. Why couldn't he be happy with after-work rendezvous and maybe some stolen kisses? Heated kisses, of course, the kind that you could feel throughout your entire body until your skin seared together. His skin my skin, my skin his skin, celestial stars meeting and shooting at each point of connection, the number of which were in the millions, all at once. A delightful shudder rippled through me, leaving behind muscles of putty. It must be all the dancing. I was exhausted. "Of course not."

"Marin Greene, I would really like to take you to the dance."

I laughed. "No."

"Why? Did someone ask you already?"

"No, I'm just not going."

"Not at all?"

"Right."

I didn't do relationships. Not only did I have no time, but my mother was miserable in relationships, and her mother before her. My grandma had been so miserable, in fact, that she'd gotten a divorce in a time when no one got divorced, and my mom said it only made her *more* miserable. Suicidal, even. Back when the only thing worse than getting a divorce was being suicidal.

I got in my car and opened the window, wondering if

there was a way to kiss him without promising anything.

He leaned in. "Who I want is not going to change."

"What if who you want doesn't want you?"

"What if she does?" He rested his forehead against the top edge of my open window. "I think she does."

I stared at him. Debated. And couldn't help it. Pressing my mouth to his, I sucked him in, fed until I hoped I would be satiated, then let go, my bottom lip lingering last.

Even separated, though, it felt like we were breathing the same breath. One. And two. And three. And four. Heaving the exhale, recovering.

"That's all she wants," I was finally able to whisper. "No dances. No dates. No boyfriends." And I started the car, put it in reverse.

He stumbled back, still in what I could only guess was shock, and let me go.

I drove home, shaky. Shaken. What was a girl to do on a Friday night when her best friend was out with a man, and her body was wondering how it could get another of those kisses?

Whirling colors had exploded across my senses, no lie. Hormones were a bitch.

Anyway, this girl went home and pored over her college essay for the fifty-seventh time, anything to keep her mind on task and *not* thinking about the yellow flowers. Big, fat petals of silky satin that I could close my eyes and crawl into, cuddle up to, and cling against.

Love was a slippery eel, the definition of it being that hard to nail down. I didn't think highly of it. Sure, I'd like to entertain the thought that the fated happily-ever-afters were out there, but honestly, romance couldn't live on, geared up to that heady height, day after day, forever. Life got in the way. People got in the way. You got in the way of yourself all the time, so how could you not get in the way of another person, even if you loved them?

I picked up my phone to text Whit and ask her who she'd really loved, of all her boyfriends, but couldn't hit the send button. The last thing I could handle right now was her trying to tell me she was in love with this hard-angled brute because he had a car.

Throwing my phone on my bed, I turned back to my desk, jumping when it pinged that I'd received a text. Maybe things had gone poorly. Maybe she needed to be rescued. Maybe she'd come to her senses.

It wasn't her.

The pad of my finger held the notification of Sam's message for a long moment before exposing it and this new level we'd reached: texting outside of work. Though, I guess his invasion of the dance studio had blown through the cieling.

>**i just realized what you were dancing to tonight**
>**anguish and HOPE**

    that doesn't mean you should have any<

>that's not what i'm saying

what are you saying<
>you pulled anguish and creepy out of the hat
>you decided on mine
>why

Without answering, I left my phone on the bed, snuffed out under a comforter. Earbuds in my ears, volume as loud as it would go without hurting, fingers on my laptop keyboard, forcing out words. This is what mattered. Dancing for the rest of my life mattered. Getting free of this house and the woman who ruled it, that was what mattered. I would not let anything stop me. And I couldn't get distracted, either.

It was a definite no to Sam.

Chapter 9

Either volunteer…

I NEARLY HAD A panic attack myself on Sunday morning when Sam pulled up in my driveway. I'd forgotten all about our plans to go to the shelter after Hannah was rushed to the hospital.

We'd learned our competition jazz choreo on Saturday without her while she rested at home with Jon, Sam, and a few of the other guys. They watched *Britain Bakes!* and tried to copy recipes from the show. Jon had pulled off a pretty impressive French tart by the time the team got there after choreo with pizzas, which was about the time Sam left for work.

Wrapping my jacket around me now, I walked out to Sam's driver's side door. He rolled his window down.

With a wince, I said, "I don't think you should come today."

"Why not?"

Glancing up at my house, I tried to find the words to explain how I was feeling. "I told Hannah in the hospital we'd go to Homecoming as a group."

"You told her..." He furrowed his brow. "After you told me yes?"

"After she had a heart attack."

"She didn't have a heart attack."

"Fine. Whatever. She needs heart surgery, Sam."

"I can't believe this."

"She's my best friend. She needs me right now."

"She always needs you, Marin. What about what you need?"

"I don't need a boyfriend," I snapped. "If that's what you mean. I can very well exist without a love interest."

He smirked at the word love, but not in a nice way. "Fine."

And that was the moment I realized he owned a piece of me now, too. He could pull the strings on my guilt as surely as Hannah and my mom.

When his window began to close, I caught it. He let his finger drop from the button but didn't look at me. Jaw set, he stared ahead.

"Don't be like that," I pleaded. Or was I pleading with myself?

"Don't be like what?" He narrowed his eyes at me. "You want me to be happy when I'm not, want me to pretend that doesn't hurt—that you can't hurt me—just so it's easier for you? Who does that?"

I do, I wanted to say, but the words got caught in my throat.

He looked away again. "My motto is: don't make Marin do anything she doesn't want to do. So I guess we're not going to the dance together."

"Has that always been your motto?" I asked, now desperate to soothe him. "Because I remember you making me eat grasshoppers in second grade."

"I'm not sorry about that," he grumbled, but his face softened a little. "You rocked that. Coolest girl in the class."

I sank into that but tried not to let a smile show on the outside.

"You know what, Marin?"

"What, Sam?"

"I'm still going today. You said they needed people. Want a ride, or no?"

I stood there, my hand on his window, rubbing my fingertip along the edge, and decided I wasn't going to do this until Hannah was out of surgery. Her life was on hold, so mine could be, too. She was my best friend and open-heart surgery was a big deal.

Honestly, she was more than my best friend. She was more like a sister. Being an only child was sometimes like living on an island where no one could reach you—or if they did, they couldn't understand you. There was no one growing up in the same house to bounce things off, to ask what was weird or unfair or out of line. You just had to guess. And that got warped by your parents' influence. If they acted like something was normal, how could you know if it wasn't? And who would you ask, anyway? Isolated. A team of one—lonely, perpetually—until that loneliness felt more like home than anything.

My life had been less lonely because of Hannah. I had perspective because I had Hannah.

"I'll see you there," I told him, and headed back up to the house.

When I got to the shelter, Sam had already been assigned to the storage room, so I requested donations. This way, we wouldn't have to interact. But then lunchtime hit.

Not only were we both serving food, but Jack put us right next to each other.

When the cute guy with floppy blond hair that I'd made the mistake of telling my mom was cute walked up and gave me a brilliant smile, I wondered how awful it would be to flirt with him in front of Sam. Whitney had always said that the best way to get over one boy was to get on someone else. But Troy's smile did nothing for me, and he definitely had a smile on him. Sam's, on the other hand...

It was times like these I really wished my mom was

right about hormones—that they were not discerning and would take anyone set in front of a horny teenager.

"Morning, Marin."

I smiled and dished noodles onto his plate. "Morning, Troy."

"How long you here for today?" he asked. Sometimes I played cribbage with him, his mom, and his little brother. He was determined to make sure his brother was taught two-person as well as four. A way to hold onto his dad's memory, I guess.

"I have to go to yoga with my mom after this."

"Some other time, then."

I nodded, and he moved along to Sam, who dumped a ladle of spaghetti sauce onto the pile of noodles.

A few more people came through before I let out a heavy sigh. "Does Jon still like Hannah?"

"Of course," he muttered. "Everyone but me still likes Hannah."

He was very intent on his ladle and the line, but was tossing only half-hearted smiles at everyone as they passed, which wasn't like him. I felt like I'd stolen the missing half.

"Why don't you still like her?" I asked softly.

"Because I see the hold she has on you and it's not fair."

"Not fair to you?"

"No. I couldn't give a shit about me right now. It's not fair to you."

"We should probably both be giving a shit about Hannah

right now, to be honest."

"Of course I give a shit about Hannah, but she will be fine. And her health has nothing to do with how you continually give up what you want for what she can't have anyway."

"Don't you know what a big deal it is to go for your best friend's crush?"

"Is that how you're spinning this? That you're the bad guy?"

Instead of replying, I forced out a big smile at Peggy, knowing she'd only get a weak one from Sam. What was I supposed to say to that? I *was* the bad guy in this situation. Maybe not usually, but this time, absolutely.

"The noodles smell good," Peggy said.

"They do?" Did noodles even smell? *Oh*, but it was a hint. Right. Noodles to plate. "Is Ron with you this morning?"

She batted a hand at me and moved over to sniff the vat of sauce in front of Sam. "Nah. He's got a new girlfriend."

A few more plops of noodles and sauce, and a handful more of Sam's half-hearted smiles before he set the ladle in the sauce and turned to me. "You're not the bad guy, Marin. You couldn't be the bad guy if you tried."

"You know, she really hates being alone. And she can't do much right now, because of her heart. And I'm busy—the whole dance team is busy. Like yesterday, when I couldn't be with her because we were learning choreo, and this morning and this afternoon..."

"That doesn't make you a bad guy. It makes you not her nurse."

"But she wants a nurse. I guarantee she wants a nurse."

"Is that why you asked about Jon? Want me to put him on her as a nurse?"

Another fifteen people came through while I chewed on this. Jon was the most sculpted guy in school. He was charming and funny and we now knew he made a mean French tart. Maybe, with enough exposure—if he showed up for her when I couldn't—maybe she'd fall for him and then I could have Sam.

Maybe it would make me feel better if I knew someone was waiting on her hand and foot while she had to lay low for sake of stress—physical and mental. And then we'd see, once her surgery came and she'd recovered, how it all played out.

"I don't think that's the worst idea," I finally admitted, smiling pure innocence at the man in line as I doled out more noodles. "He might be able to win her over with food. Tell him to bake—a lot. She prefers butterscotch chips in her cookies and chocolate cake over vanilla."

Sam smiled but didn't say anything. Five more people, ten.

"If he wants to bring her flowers, she prefers them in white. Any kind of flower, as long as they're white."

He looked at me, slyly, as if we were plotting something. But we weren't. It wasn't like that. I was just making sure she was well cared for while she was down. Her parents were great, but her mom didn't bake unless it was Christmas, and her dad was allergic to flowers. She had to keep them in her room with the door closed. She loved them, though—they'd be a treat.

"And besides *Britain Bakes!* she loves rom-coms and old horror films."

Sam's grin brightened back to full wattage and my own probably looked really flirtatious, because though it wasn't facing Sam, it was because of him, and for him, and about him.

Maybe, even if Homecoming was a bust, things could work out after all.

I went straight to the yoga studio, which had been a mistake. I got there early, and my mom was at the desk. Smiling as I walked in, she patted the seat beside her.

"How was the shelter?"

"Good."

"Troy and his mom still there?"

"And his little brother, yes." I pulled my hair up into

a messy bun for class. I'd worn yoga pants and a sports bra under my baggy sweatshirt so I wouldn't have to change. And now we could welcome everyone in and take their money while pretending we were the perfect mother/daughter duo.

Reaching behind me, my mom yanked the messy bun out, pulling at my hair enough to make me flinch.

"Ow!"

"Braid it. It's going to bother you in class if it's not flat down the back of your head."

"It's high enough it won't bother me." I grabbed the rubber band back from her and wound it up again.

"It looks neater braided, Marin. And it will bother you. Trust me."

I looked at her in challenge. "You want it braided so badly, you braid it."

She huffed. We both knew she couldn't, because she didn't know how. The first time she'd left me at a haircut alone, I'd asked the lady to teach me. It was my first secret—not the first time my mother had disappointed me, but the first time I realized I didn't need her, that I could figure it out on my own.

"You were always quite self-sufficient," she muttered, clearly having drawn up the same memory.

"I had to be."

She studied me. "You're saying it's my fault?"

"Of course not." That would only start a fight.

"So you're just being mean?"

I took in a deep breath of air and counted to three, then let it out.

She crossed her arms. "You must get that from your father."

"Being mean?" I laughed. "Because I couldn't have learned it from you?"

In a rare moment of self-reflection, she replied, "Sometimes my honesty comes out mean, but I always intend it with love."

I snorted. "You're saying it's okay to be mean as long as you're being honest?"

"Would you rather I be inauthentic? Would you rather have a mother who pretends?"

"I'd rather have a mother who didn't tell me all the reasons she didn't like me—all the ways I do everything wrong."

It was silent for a moment, but for the heater kicking in to warm up the hot yoga room and the music wafting gently from the speakers in the ceiling. The space between us grew. It was painful, such a great expanse wedging itself into such a small proximity. The lobby couldn't hold us. The studio couldn't hold us. A mansion couldn't hold us. With a hand to my suddenly tight throat, I stood and walked into the hallway for air.

"You don't like me, either," she said, her voice trailing me like an afterthought.

Deep lungfuls of breaths. Well, at least I didn't have to guess anymore. At least now I knew.

"You think I'm strict," she called through the glass door that was propped open. "Moody. Needy."

Controlling, dramatic, and suffocating, but it was close. I turned to look at her but didn't retrace my steps.

"I used to be strong and independent. Full of life. Then I got married."

I prayed this wasn't going where I thought it was going. I did not need to hear about how men can ruin your life—not when I was just starting to hope that something might be able to come of Sam and me. *Please just let me be happy today. It might not last very long, anyway.*

"It's not your dad's fault. I'm not saying that. I'm saying that if you try to hold on too tight to what you are, so much that you refuse to learn from someone else, you can lose yourself as easily as you can lose yourself from becoming what they want you to be. Dig your heels in and stagnancy puts you back, you know?"

She was waiting for me to get it, but I didn't. And I didn't get why she seemed to be confessing something now, when her clients were about to stream in and coo over her. Did she want me to be screaming into the madness when they did?

"Maybe together we could have figured out a good balance. Maybe if we could have taught each other something, instead of refusing to be taught, maybe things would have turned out differently."

"If you hadn't gotten divorced, you mean?"

"Right."

"Or," I reasoned, "maybe you would've been miserable forever."

"I guess there's no way to know."

I walked back and stood by the chair I'd been sitting in. "Do you wish you wouldn't have gotten divorced?"

She looked up at me thoughtfully. "I'm glad I got divorced because it got to a point where I couldn't stop trying to control him. I thought if I could make him do what I wanted, we'd be happy. I thought I knew what happiness was. But you can't control happiness. I may not have found it yet, but I've figured that much out. So, I'm glad I'm free of that. I'm not sure I ever would have been able to stop trying to force it if I'd stayed."

I could remember how that felt, the force of her back then. Not that it felt much different than the force of her now. I got more of it—all of it, maybe—but if my parents had still been married, Dad would've probably taken the brunt of it. This was why I thought he'd wanted out, because it made a person feel desperate, being enmeshed with her. And there was no other way, because she demanded enmeshment (points four, five, and six of contention).

All or nothing—and since she was my mother, I didn't have the choice of nothing. She clung, she fed, she *took*.

Backing out of that sticky mental compartment, I asked, "Dad didn't want the divorce?" I remembered feeling like she wanted to escape us, but I guess he had to have wanted out as well.

"He did, he just wouldn't have instigated it. He was as miserable as me, but too loyal to admit it. Anyway. At the same time, I'm *not* glad I got divorced, since it means I won't have anyone left when you go to college."

"You just admitted you don't really like me."

"I may not like you, but I love you. And I want to be around when you grow up. Once the world teaches you some lessons, then we can really have something."

So many chances for her to rewind the clock and pay attention to what she's saying, how she's saying it, the message she's sending.

I don't like you, but once you learn some harsh world lessons, I'm hoping I will then.

Locking my jaw in place, I stalked to the bathroom. "I'll get everything ready in the studio," I called back behind me.

Her past pleas echoed in my head: *I lived in a very chaotic home, my mom was all I had, inside her I was safe, I can't help who I am, I'm still hurting, it still hurts. Be gentle with me.* And even though she wasn't actually saying it now, the strings in my heart began to unravel, the tug of them anchoring me to someone else's desires dragging me under again.

But would staying here for college accomplish anything?

There was no way to make her feel better. Nothing I'd ever done or said made her feel better. So why keep trying? Even if I let her embed herself in my skin like she'd been in her mother's, I didn't think that would make her happy, either. And it would definitely destroy me. Besides, none of it was because she loved me, not really. It was because she needed me to hold her up.

Inside what she wanted, I was ultimately expendable.

Closing the door quietly, I slid to the floor and soaked in the overwhelming heat. I had at least fifteen minutes, and it might take me that long to recover from such a realization.

It was my own mother who made me weaker.

Chapter 10

...or work.

I PULLED INTO MY normal spot next to Sam's truck, which he was leaning against with arms and legs crossed. According to the schedule, we'd be working the exact same shift today, and he'd clearly been waiting for me.

"Hi, Sam," I said, getting out of my car.

"The elusive Marin Greene," he quipped, jumping into step next to me. "Kissing boys and running away."

"I've been busy."

"But today, tonight?" He opened the door for me, the one that led us into the back of the store near the time clock.

"Property of Fiesta Grocers until nine," I said, motioning up and down over an outfit that matched his—black pants, white collared shirt, royal-blue tie.

"After that?"

The door swung shut behind me. I had to blink a few times, my eyes adjusting to the dark walls and darker steel shelving. "After that, I figured I'd do what I normally do after work."

"Hang out with me and Kesh?"

Biting the inside of my cheek, I snatched my timesheet, punched in, and spun away from him. "Except Kesh won't be here, because I'm working for him."

Which meant what? What would happen after work? What did I want to happen?

I'd told him I wouldn't go to the dance, but that kiss... I could picture it: us in his truck in the parking lot, steam sizzling out through the exhaust, through the window and door seams. An oasis I could enjoy and walk away from, a magical place that only existed here, on these nights, within reach of work.

Our assistant manager yelled my name from the swinging silver door that led out to the store. I was needed up front to cover the service desk lunches, which meant I had a few hours to dissect this new lurching of my stomach every time Sam walked by.

Or maybe that was just the smell of the store today, which was a little more rotten produce than fresh bakery and cardboard.

After the service desk lunches were complete, I was sent to the registers. It was always ten times busier there, so that was a bit of a distraction until Sam came up with two cases of water to help an old lady who'd forgotten a cart.

Shuffling both cases to one arm while I scanned them, he slipped a note to me while the woman paid.

Kesh not working means it's just you and me, right? I really want to talk to you.

After thinking about it a minute, I wrote, *I really want to kiss you,* and folded it over his timecard when I punched out for lunch.

I walked across the street to Sub Stop and, back at work about the time he should be going on his lunch break, received a texted response: I really want you to go to the dance with me.

I sighed, got a look from our general manager, and made myself busy.

At eight o'clock, I was sent to help Sam finish stocking canned vegetables in aisle four and found him with a barnacle attached to his foot. Hannah was sitting cross-legged next to him, fingers in her luscious hair—she was always playing with it like that to keep it from getting too tangled—and spinning hypnosis with her twirling eyes, trying to convince him to go to the movies after work.

"But we picked the late one, just for you."

His eyes cut over to me, and hers followed. "I think I have plans," he said, turning back to the tomato sauce.

"Come on, Sam, pretty please-me with fun on top?"

Ugh. I'd always hated that. *Pretty please-me.* I pulled out my box cutter and threw it with precision into the shelf between them, two centimeters from her perfectly perfect nose. Or, I sliced the canned corn box open, imagining that it was her outer shell and peeling back the layers would reveal the girl I used to know.

"I really can't, Hannah," he said for—and I was making

an educated guess here—the five-hundredth time. The girl was nothing if not persistent.

"Fine." She said it with her chin on her knees, the way she used to sit when we watched scary movies. "Can you at least help me find the iron supplements?"

"They're in aisle ten."

"You aren't going to ask why I need them?"

"He's not," I muttered. "Because the world doesn't revolve around you."

Sam shot a squinty, confused glance in my direction.

"He was my friend before he was yours," she snapped at me, clambering to her feet. "Forget it. I'll find them myself, but just so you know, in case you were worried about an old friend"—only, she was staring at him, not me—"I'm *not* fine, I'm anemic!"

And then she didn't go anywhere. I rolled my eyes. "Anemia is not that big a deal."

She glared at me. "Says the girl who thinks no one's problems are bigger than her own."

"Guys!" Sam's eyes were about as wide as his head.

I waved a hand at them and moved down ten feet to do the green beans.

Sam struggled to his feet, stuck in the small space between Hannah and his dolly. "Anemia can be a big deal if it's related to something more serious," he said, placating her for me, which was completely unnecessary.

"I wasn't eating very well because of stress due to my

heart condition, you know." This time she was glaring at me, but her gluttonous hair seemed to reach out for Sam with its sticky, webbed fingers. I glared back at her. But—heart condition?

"It's aisle ten," Sam said, stepping between us. "I'll show you."

They were gone for a while, longer than it took to find the pharmacy aisle and long enough for me to finish my boxes and start on his. When I was down to three cans left, he snuck up behind me. Hand resting on the dolly, he wasted no time: "What was that all about?"

I sighed. "She didn't tell you?"

"You know she was just in the hospital, right? She's having an ablation surgery next week."

With a frown, I shook my head. "Of course I didn't know that. What's an ablation surgery?"

"She thought she was having panic attacks, but Friday after halftime, she collapsed. Apparently, she has an extra pathway in her heart." Cue his serious face. Unfortunately, it was something I was really starting to like, polished and smooth.

"That doesn't sound good. She's having *heart surgery?*" Shit. I was an asshole.

"It actually seems pretty simple. They go up the groin through a vein and *voila*. No cuts, no sedation even. So again, I ask, what was that all about? I didn't even know you guys knew each other."

Looking away, I frowned. "We used to be best friends. And I mean *best*—Whitney and her and me. Then she got too good for us."

He crouched down to eye level, the smooth intent of his expression now pinching to concern. I wanted to reach out and smooth the crease between his eyebrows. "Marin, no one is too good for you."

I huffed out my amusement. "Thanks, Sam, but I don't need to be reassured." Standing, I grabbed my dolly and headed across the store. He followed me with his. Watching the floor, the tiles whooshing beneath me, I listened for his feet and the wheels behind him, not letting him get too far behind, or too close.

Our assistant manager was in back crushing boxes and told us we could go, so we punched out and emerged into the chilly fall wind.

Kesh was waiting for us in a hoody and fleece with a bottle of whiskey.

"Hey!" I cried, like a crow had gotten caught in my throat. Surprise hopefully masked the disappointment of thwarted alone time with Sam, which I didn't—okay, *shouldn't*—want. "What're you doing here?"

"I missed you guys."

Sam and I looked at each other, and I admitted to myself that this was probably a message from the universe.

"You brought the hard stuff," Sam noted. He sat down next to Kesh and took a sip, made a face, then spit it out.

I frowned. "You guys know it's cold out here, right?"

"It was almost fifty today." Kesh scooted over and patted the space between them. "Can't be under forty right now. We'll keep you warm."

"Whiskey, too," Sam added, lifting the bottle up, "will keep you warm."

I raised an eyebrow. Sam generally turned down the alcohol. Maybe we could both toe the line tonight. I smiled. "Kisses would keep me warmer."

"Damn you, girl," Sam muttered, taking another swig from the bottle and forcing it down this time with a shudder.

I grinned and took the vape Kesh was handing me with a raised eyebrow. "You two have finally gone there?" he asked.

"Don't be sad," I ran a hand up and down his arm for reassurance as Sam handed him the bottle. "I love you, too."

Kesh had been mid-drink, and this sent him coughing. Wiping off his mouth with the back of his hand, he recovered. "You know I like guys, right?"

"No," I admitted. "That is not something I knew."

"Yeah." Kesh leaned back. "Only guys."

"But you kissed me once," I remembered, thinking back to one of my first high school parties freshman year.

"And you kissed me. But you heart Sam here."

My eyes widened in his direction so he'd know to shut

it with that kind of talk. Then I forced myself to recover. "Sam and I are undefined and undefinable."

Kesh raised a smirk in my direction, then handed me the bottle. "You guys coming to my party next weekend? Starts at the same time as the Homecoming dance, for those of us boycotting."

"I'm boycotting," I said lightly. "I'll grab Whit and hopefully not her stupid boyfriend. Have I told you guys about him?"

Sam frowned. Yeah, so I'd crushed him a bit. That's why I'd wanted to stick to kisses. Kisses didn't crush anyone, they just existed. Better to accept what was *now* and find happiness in that than to stress over what could be, only to discover it might have the power to destroy you.

Sam offered me the bottle. I shook my head and Sam reached farther to give it to Kesh. I already felt heightened and woozy, like I was swimming through liquid anti-depressants. At least, that's how I'd always imagined an anti-depressant would feel, back when I'd first found my mom's pill bottle and she'd tried to explain them.

It was the feeling of new beginnings I was riding on. More kisses and new thrills. Beginnings were the sweet spot, when the sunlight was still streaming through the window and you could taste the hope in the air. I always tried to keep it right there, in the beginning, because hope evaporated pretty quickly. Then the darkness resettled and you found your mom unconscious on the floor.

I pulled my phone out of my pocket.

party at Kesh's the night of the dance<
>kesh's brother is friends with vic

vic is not invited<
>ikik
>don't worry
>he doesn't know I'm still in hs anyway

I blinked multiple times at my phone. So that was even more concerning, but I supposed a point for him.

how old does he think you are<
>i do want you two to hang out sometime soon tho
WHIT<
how old does he think you are??<

She didn't reply. Minutes ticked by, Kesh and Sam chatting around me. I refused to answer her until she answered me. And I refused to hang out with him until he knew she was in high school. Eventually, Sam nudged me with his elbow.

"You okay?" he asked.

I grabbed Kesh's bottle and took a long-overdue, searing drink to burn my soul.

Kesh grinned. "Thatta girl."

"I thought you weren't drinking." Sam tried to take it

from me, but I jerked it back and took another sip, wiping my mouth with the back of my hand and squeezing my eyes shut as I handed it over. "Marin..."

"Friend problems, Sam. You're driving now."

"This about Whit's boyfriend?"

"Guys. He's *twenty-five*. She can't be serious, right?"

"Well, he can't be," Kesh agreed.

"Hey! Get me some dirt, Kesh. His name is Vic. She said he's friends with your brother."

"Vic what?"

"I have no idea. Isn't Vic enough? He's bald and really beefy, wears polos, and runs a lot."

"Oh. I think I've met him."

"And?"

Kesh shrugged. "He's a nice guy. I'm kind of surprised he'd go for a high schooler."

"Yes, well. He doesn't know she's a high schooler."

Kesh and I shared a look.

"Maybe don't be the one to break it to him," I added.

"My parents were seven years apart," Sam said.

Swinging my gaze to him, I said, "You're supposed to be on my side, Sam. Not hers. And definitely not the twenty-five-year-old's."

"I get it. You're worried. You should be. I'm just saying when something's right, it's right."

"No," I clipped. "When something *seems* right, it often falls apart."

"Well, this night is taking a turn," he mumbled.

I studied him. His hair was getting a little longer, which meant unruly, and his jaw was tight. He'd wanted a date and a kiss and a promise of a dance. I couldn't give him all that, but I could give him some of it. Our desires did have an intersection.

"Okay, Sam. Time to drive me home."

"I just had a drink."

"Then time to sober up in your truck with me before you take me home." I hopped off the dock and reached for his hand. He let my fingers slide through his, and in that instant, it was like a vacuum had sealed around us, the world shrink-wrapping tight until we were all that was left.

Kesh raised an eyebrow and took a swig of his whiskey, then hopped down next to me, kissed me on the cheek, and ambled off in the direction of his house.

I tugged Sam along to his truck, opened his door, got him settled in, buckled his seatbelt with a wink, and then waltzed around to the passenger side. By the time I was settled, he had the engine on, the heat turned up, and the radio set low and moody.

Sliding over next to him on the bench seat, I lifted a hand to his face and turned his head toward me. "I'm going to kiss you now."

"No, you're not."

"Sam. This can work out for both of us, I promise. We

don't have to have a relationship to have some fun."

"Marin, no." He unbuckled himself and got out of the car, slamming the door and leaning against it so all I could see was the back of his head.

That whiskey had made me tired. I rested my head against the seat and closed my eyes. My feet were finally bathed in warmth and my nose didn't feel so cold, which meant I was not getting out of this truck to talk to him.

When the door opened, I startled. Maybe I'd drifted off a bit.

"I want you the right way," he said, standing outside and letting all the cold air in. "Not the wrong way."

"There's no wrong way to have me," I told him, motioning him inside.

"I'm taking you home." Running a hand over his head, he stopped it on the back curve of his neck and held it there a moment. "We can talk about this tomorrow."

Rolling my eyes, I slid over to the far window. Talking about this was exactly what I didn't want to do.

The ride home was quiet because I didn't want to talk, and he didn't want to kiss me. Or he did, but not without talking, and that was my deal-breaker.

He was right. The night had taken a turn. I got out of his truck without looking back, unable to face his disappointment, knowing I wouldn't be able to resist his pout.

My own disappointment? I was well accustomed to that.

When I walked into the dark kitchen, my mom's silhouette greeted me from a chair pulled out in the middle of the room. Great. Just what I needed.

"Mother," I greeted, locking the door behind me.

"Marin," she replied. "Where were you?"

"Drinking with Sam."

"Drinking gets girls pregnant."

"Penises ejaculating inside girls is what gets them pregnant."

"Where'd you get such a nasty mouth?" She said it with the tone that let me know she was looking for a fight.

My muscles coiled, and every bit of me felt like springs, ready to jump. This, my choice, hung in the air between us—fight back or back down. I noted it every time but could never force myself to fold to her will or her needs or her ways.

I got out one loud word and she jumped in louder. We were both yelling. I was going on about how I was early and didn't need to tell her where I was every second and she was a terrible excuse for a mother. She was going on about how dare I talk back to her and how was she supposed to protect me if I was never honest with her and I was a lousy excuse for a daughter.

Oh, I knew how lousy I was. She didn't waste one minute telling me what a shit I was to her, or what a shit I was in general. What I couldn't understand is why it was my responsibility to be the bigger, better, more mature person when she was the parent.

Then my dad walked in.

He didn't need to say anything to shut us up. All it took was the tousled hair to know we'd woken the sleeping bear.

"Sorry, Dad."

"It's fine, Matt."

His hand motioned toward the microwave. "She's not late."

"No."

"Then what's the problem?"

My mom pointed at me. "She's disrespectful."

I snorted. "She's unreasonable."

"Marin, to the table. Elizabeth, go to bed."

She let out what could only be described as a growl before stomping off.

My dad flopped down on a kitchen chair but didn't say anything until we heard the slam of their bedroom door. Pressing his fingers to either side of his nose, he said, "Haven't you learned yet, to play the game? You don't fight back, and she can't make it into anything."

I dropped my purse on the table and sat down. "If I don't fight back, she wins."

"Do you feel like you're winning?"

I squirmed in my seat. No, of course not. But fighting sometimes felt like winning.

The light from the moon was sweeping through the window at an angle, a corner of it on his face and the rest on the floor beyond him. I studied this beyond-him part for a minute, thinking about how he followed his own advice—not fighting—and wondering where that had gotten him. Because they were miserable.

"Why don't you leave?" I wondered. If he wouldn't fight her, why not leave her? Wouldn't that be better than this?

My dad set both elbows on the table, letting his hands drop across to mine. Deep breath in, hard exhale out. "I remember who she was. I promised that woman. I loved her. And I keep hoping she'll come back."

"She won't."

"Don't lose hope, Marin. You have nothing left if you don't have hope."

I chewed on my lip a minute, but something about the night, the deep navy of the sky outside and the soft whisper of the moonlight dancing across the room, something about it all felt secret, and sacred, creating a moment where anything could be said.

So, I said it: "And what if, fifty years from now, you're sitting in your chair with the newspaper, and you realize she never came back. All that time, wasted."

He shook his head at me. "Nothing's wasted on hope."

"Dad." I leaned over the table as far as it would allow. "I guarantee you being single would be better than this."

"Shh." He patted my hands, which were warming under his. "Any other woman I'd find, we'd have problems, too. At least I know what these particular problems are."

"I didn't say with another woman. I said single. No complications, utter freedom."

"Honey, there are always complications, no matter if you're in a relationship or not. Can't get away from that."

I dropped my head to the table in resignation. What was the point of all this trouble trying to stay out of a relationship if Sam brought me complications anyway? He did, too. He was in my face, causing problems, and didn't seem likely to go away. Or hadn't, before tonight. I was guessing he was gone for good now, though.

My dad slapped a hand down on the wood and stood. "Come on. Let's go to sleep."

"You're not going to yell at me for being disrespectful?"

"I did. Back when I said, 'how come you never learn to play the game?'"

I followed him up the stairs, wishing we had more talks like this. Well, not like this, but just talks. More Dad in my life and less Mom. But when he wasn't busy with work, he was sort of shut down, which is what I was afraid of, I guess. If I gave up the fight, would I end up numb and defeated, too?

And was my dad trapped because he'd rather have hope than be single? Or was I trapped because I'd rather be single than have hope?

Chapter 11
Either extra credit...

HANNAH WASN'T AT SCHOOL.

Normally, she'd have told me the night before that her mom was letting her stay home. Or texted me in the middle of the night when she threw up. Or whined on a video message about how bad her head hurt.

Maybe she'd just slept in. It happened occasionally. But now, with the heart condition, my hackles were up.

I didn't actually think about it first hour, because it was a B Day and she never came in for first hour on B Days. Once lunch hit, though, I blew up her phone.

yo<
you sick<
everything okay<
heart thingz?<
or just sleepy<
hannah?<
whats up<

After third period, I tried to call. Straight to voicemail.

My knee wouldn't stop bouncing under the table during fourth, and as soon as the bell rang, I was out the door.

"Marin?" Mr. Ellis called. "Can I talk to you for a minute?"

I contained a groan, my mind elsewhere, which is probably what he wanted to talk to me about. "Yes, Mr. Ellis?"

He sat down at his desk and waited for the stampede to finish filing out of his room. "I wanted to talk to you about your recent work."

"If this is about the exam, I'm sorry. I was as shocked as you." I had gotten a C. A C! "I'll try harder next time."

"This isn't about one exam. If you want to stay in the National Honor Society, if you want to get into your top school—Wash U, is it?" He'd sent a recommendation letter for me. I nodded. "And you're thinking of a graduate degree, correct?"

I nodded again. "Physical therapy, specializing in dance injuries."

"Marin, if you start slacking now, when you have so far to go..." He shook his head and let a doomed sort of fate hang unspecified in the air between us.

"I wasn't slacking, Mr. Ellis, it's not like that. I'm sorry. I'll do better, I promise."

He studied me a moment, his brow furrowed. "Is everything okay?"

No. Nothing was okay. My best friend was having heart

surgery and I was trying very hard to keep myself away from the boy she liked. "Nothing's wrong, Mr. Ellis."

"I noticed you didn't do the extra credit." He motioned to the pile on his desk.

"I've been really busy." It took a lot of energy to keep Sam at arm's length. Especially when he was now regularly volunteering at the shelter, his shifts often overlapping with mine.

"I'll give you till morning." He tapped his desk with the eraser of his pencil. "I think it's necessary to help this grade of yours."

"Thank you." Though why I should thank him for making an optional assignment mandatory, I didn't know.

"All right. I'll see you first thing in the morning."

Great. Hannah and I had been planning to go to the soccer game, not that I had any idea where she was, but now I had too much to do.

ellis is worried about my future, I texted her. Still no response. Was it crazy of me to call her mom? Not under the circumstances, right? She did have a heart condition.

I found her in my contact list and bit my lip, but just then my phone rang.

"Hannah?"

"Hey! Hi. Sorry."

"Where are you? Are you okay?"

"Peachy. One hundred percent. Are you okay?"

"Yeah, but I can't go to the soccer game. Mr. Ellis is

making me do that extra credit."

"But it's extra, how can he make you?"

"I don't know. What's that noise?"

"Nothing, hang on." There was a shuffling and a closed door.

"Are you at the hospital?"

"No, I'm fine. But it's okay. I don't really feel like a soccer game today, either."

"You really don't mind?"

"Of course not. I'll see you Wednesday."

"Not tomorrow?"

"They adjusted my meds and I'm feeling a bit weird. Doctor says to stay home one more day and make sure all is well."

"Well, maybe I could talk my mom into letting me stay home with you."

"No, it's cool. That wouldn't fly with Mr. Ellis. Besides, I think Jon is going to."

I looked around the empty high school hallway. This was all weird. Today was weird. But if she said she was okay and didn't care if I went to the soccer game, I had extra credit and National Honor Society to worry about.

"I have to do the extra credit by tomorrow morning or Ellis is threatening to kick me out of National Honor Society."

"No need for that if we go to KU."

"I'm only going to KU if I don't get in anywhere else." Because the whole point of college, to me—how many times did I have to say it?—was to get away from my mother.

"Yeah, yeah. I'm just teasing."

"But you're not. That's the problem. And if you keep bringing it up, then I'm making you apply to Wash U. There's still time."

"Marin, you know I can't get into Wash U."

"Doesn't mean you can't apply, just in case."

She sighed. "Maybe I will, depending on how my surgery turns out."

I froze, a hand in my locker, the hall around me still. "Are you saying if you're not *dead* after surgery, you'll apply?"

"Only two percent of people die from heart surgery, and three percent have complications."

"But most of them are old, Hannah. Old and sick with diabetes or other preexisting conditions." We'd done our homework together, on her bed, to an episode of *Britain Bakes!* that she'd already watched without me. With Jon.

"Exactly."

"I can't believe you're so chill about this." Ever since they'd diagnosed her, she'd been her old self again. Knowing what it was, she said, made all the difference in the world. Plus, she was on meds that were supposed to help keep things under control until her surgery. But I couldn't get over the fact that she was having heart surgery. At seventeen.

"No use worrying about it until there's a reason to worry

about it, right?"

"Right." A silence drew out as I tried to put my finger on what was wrong about this conversation.

"We're still going to Homecoming as a group?" she asked.

"That was the plan." I bit my lip, chewed on it for a moment. "Why? Do you want to go with Jon?"

"Why would you think I'd want to go with Jon?"

"Because you're picking him tomorrow instead of me."

"Or is it because you want to go with Sam?" she asked.

Of course I wanted to go with Sam. She shouldn't need to ask. "I am going with Sam," I pointed out. "So are you."

"You know what I mean. He asked you, didn't he? Jon said he asked you."

I tried to tell her I'd said yes, that Sam and I had been on the cusp of making a plan before she went down in that hallway. But when it came to loosing the words from my tongue, I simply couldn't say them. Instead, I told her, "You're more important to me than any boy."

"You're more important to me than anything," she replied.

"Okay, I'm going to go home and do my homework, and then we'll video chat later, okay?"

"I'll probably be asleep. Seriously, these new meds..."

"Why are you on new meds, though? Did you have another arrythmia?"

"The old ones were just giving me too many side effects."

"But you've been fine."

"I gotta go, okay? I'll talk to you tomorrow night."

"Tomorrow night?"

And then she hung up. What in the actual hell? I crossed my arms and tapped my fingertips along my phone. She was keeping something from me. But if that something was Jon, I didn't really want to unearth it. Let that happen. Let her get so into Jon that she couldn't deny me Sam any longer.

Still... I flipped through to the map on my app and tried to find her. We always had our locations on for each other, but she was nowhere to be found. Had she and Jon gone away for the night or something? Would her parents even let her, considering her heart? Or maybe they let her precisely because of her heart...before her surgery.

Mr. Ellis walked out of his room then, messenger bag over his shoulder, and he raised an eyebrow at me. Like he knew I was wasting time.

Right. Homework. Essays. Extra credit.

Still, the whole walk home, I tried to imagine what it would be like, having both her and Sam. If she went for Jon, if the four of us could be a thing, if she'd ever be able to watch Sam and me without hating us and hating me...

We'd always said we'd never pick a boy over a best friend. It was a pact that went back ages, to HannahWhitneyandI, and it was formed in cement. I felt bound to that still, even though she surely would have picked Sam over me last year, if he'd have had her.

My mom was in her bedroom when I got home, so I slipped into mine to work on my extra credit paper. Maybe an hour later, she appeared in the doorway, looking tired. The dying light from the windows in my room lit her up against the shadows in the hall. The freckles on her face, which I'd only gotten, like, seven of, stood out on her creamy skin and her brown hair fell in one piece over her shoulder, like she'd been twisting it all day.

"You working on those applications?" she asked.

"No. An essay for extra credit. But I can't concentrate."

"Inability to concentrate in juveniles is most often related to relations with the opposite sex." But she smiled when she said it—a relaxed one, too, nothing tight about it. "Grandma used to say that to me all the time. She made it sound technical, but I don't think it was."

I smiled. Grandma had been the type who made everything she said sound like fact.

"Are you finished with your college apps?" she asked.

"Yeah, Dad just has to pay the fees. He said he'd do it this weekend."

She slid into the room and sat on the bed. "I can do it right now."

I raised an eyebrow. She was not generally the fee-paying parent.

"You have to pay online." My mom didn't believe in opening herself up to identity theft like that, and she also didn't believe in credit cards. She had one, of course, but only for the most dire of emergencies, not so she could use it online—because that was just asking someone to snag the number and rack up fraudulent charges.

Holding her hands out for my computer, she said, "I'll sacrifice my identity this one time, for you."

I handed it over. It would feel great to have it done.

"You work on that, and I'll work on this. KU, K-State, and Wash U, right?"

I nodded.

She slid her palm over my hand. Since she wasn't much for affection, I willed myself to stay there, to stay still. Her hand on mine didn't have to mean she was holding me down.

"I don't want you to feel any pressure from me about where to go. But you *are* my only family now that Ma's gone."

Yep. Slipping my fingers out from beneath hers, I hid them under my thigh. "You're not supposed to need me, Mom. I'm supposed to need you."

"But you don't even want me, do you?" She stood, the trace of any smile or relaxed pleasantry on her face gone with the dying sun. "You don't include me in anything."

"What do you want me to include you in?"

Turning to face me but not coming back to sit, she replied, "Boys. Dance. Your life."

"You did help me narrow down my major." Though it had

been slightly torturous for me: *You can't dance for a living. How long since you've actually practiced ballet? Think business, to start your own studio. Or physical therapy, where you could help dancers with injuries. Something realistic.*

It didn't sting anymore, though. She was right.

"What's happening with the boy, Marin? How many ways do I have to ask?"

"The boy is on hold, Mom. I'm worried about Hannah right now."

We stared at each other a minute. Had she actually forgotten, or was she just trying to work her way into sympathy for another human being?

"Poor Alexia," she muttered. "I should send her a card." Stumbling out of my room and down the hall to hers, I heard her rummaging in her desk.

Sympathy for the mother. Well, I guess it was something.

Chapter 12

...or extra time.

THE BELL RANG AND we were out the door.

"Marin?" Or not.

My shoulders dropped and I turned slowly, weaving through the few people still filing out. "Yes, Mr. Ellis?"

"I know you like to skip class and put minimal effort into your homework, but your exams are usually better than this. Want to tell me what's going on?"

"I'm just busy." Dance classes and solos and work, oh my. Not to mention trying to be as available as possible to keep Whit from spending even more time with Vic. I was more than busy. More like dizzy, to be honest.

"You're a bright girl, Marin. You can make it to college if you put in a little more effort."

"I am going to college," I stated. The applications were already in—I'd sent them myself.

"If that's your plan, I don't think you can risk dropping your grades to Cs."

"It doesn't matter anymore, does it?" I didn't think Chapman was going to look at my grades this year. Didn't all seniors slack off a bit?

"I will not encourage you to merely get by." He grabbed my recent exam off the pile of books in my hand. "I'm disappointed that you thought I'd let this go."

"I didn't think anything, Mr. Ellis. I just took the exam."

"It might help your grade if you do that extra credit paper."

"It was due today," I pointed out.

"I'd be willing to give you until morning."

"No thanks, Mr. Ellis. I appreciate it and all, but I'll make sure my next exam's an A, okay?"

"Marin, I know right now your life feels confined to what happens in this small space of yours that is home and high school—rules your parents inflict on you, boys, friends, homework. But it won't be like that forever, and what you do now will make a difference then."

"Look, I could tell you I'm going to do it and then not show in the morning, because I seriously *don't have time.*" I could study while stretching but didn't think writing an essay would work quite as well. "So how about I promise to study three times as hard for the next exam?"

"And your homework? You'll start doing it again?"

"Yes. Tonight."

"In your other classes, too?"

I looked up in surprise. Was this to be the first of many conversations like this? "Fine. In all my classes."

"Then you're free to go."

I got out of there as fast as I could. He was right, which was the shitty part. Not that I could squeeze any more hours out of my day.

"I wish Mr. Ellis kept *me* after class," Whit muttered, when I caught up to her at my locker. She was leaning against it, picking her already-frayed fingernails.

Her attraction to Mr. Ellis took on a whole new meaning now, and I scowled. We'd barely talked about Vic since I'd met him at the park. Every time we'd tried, it had turned into an argument—her comparing me to all the judgmental people I hated most in the world, and me questioning her intelligence and sanity—so we'd skirted around it like experts, because ignoring each other was not an option, even when we were mad.

Why did I have so many notebooks in my locker? There had to be seven and I only remembered writing in one. Which one, though? I could use that one about now. Whit plucked out the one I needed and I gave her a look, then dug deeper in the mess for the textbooks I knew had to be there.

Closing my locker, I shrugged on my backpack, which now weighed like a million pounds. Our plan was to head to the park, but as we walked across the lot, I saw the school's soccer team warming up on the field.

"Is there a game today, or is this practice?" I asked.

Whit shrugged. "Got me."

I didn't realize I was walking slowly in that direction

until she cleared her throat from a few feet behind me.

"Are we going to the game?" she asked.

"Is it a game?"

"I don't know. Are we going?"

"Oh, no." I shook my head. "We don't do that kind of thing."

"Have you ever seen him play?"

"Not really."

She walked past me to the bleachers.

"No!" I cried. "He can't see me watching. That would only encourage him." But she was way ahead of me, and by the time I reached her, she was climbing up through the sparse crowd, yelling his name.

"Whit!" I hissed, stumbling over myself to grab her arm.

"Marin." Sam's voice, from behind me.

I froze before slowly turning around. *No, this does not mean I'm looking for a relationship.*

He rested a foot up on the first bleacher. "Are you staying for the game?"

"Oh, I'm sure not. Whitney just wanted to watch you warm up."

She snorted. Surely, he wasn't that stupid, although he did take the time to send Whit a curious glance. "Maybe we could talk after?" he asked.

Before I could reply, his coach was yelling for him. As he jogged back onto the field, I turned to Whit, mortified. "I can't talk to him. We have to get out of here."

"We have plenty of time." She sat down. "And you, like this, are too much fun to watch."

"Me like what?" I cried.

"Human, like the rest of us, with feelings for a *boy*." Her tone was strange, though. "Maybe you'll understand me when your feelings for Sam get so strong you can't help but fall into it."

I plopped down, knocking into her. She winced, like I'd hit a bruise, and I raised an eyebrow at her.

"It's nothing. I just stepped in at the wrong time." She yanked on a chunk of her ghostly white hair, running her spindly fingers down the skyscraper length of it and spinning the end into a sharp point. "Miri was fighting with both of them, screaming about something stupid, totally out of control. I was trying to pull her out—she was just working them up more—and Mom shoved an end table over. My hip caught the corner, and I caught the lamp." She made a face. "Everything is still in one piece."

Her parents tended to break things, not usually people. Even so, the noise in that house, the screaming, was enough to give me a tic. "Let's find some cheap, crappy apartment next month when you turn eighteen. We'll get a couch for Miri, and I can go to KU."

"No way. You want to get out."

"KU has automatic scholarships that would help me with rent. It's a win-win. Besides, Mr. Ellis now has me convinced I won't get into Chapman because I'm a slacker."

"You're not a slacker, and I'm not going to hold you back. You're going to L.A."

I leaned my head back and closed my eyes. The studios there... What I could learn from the choreographers both at Chapman and in L.A. was next level.

Whit hooked a finger through one of the many ratty friendship bracelets on my wrist, most of which she'd made or stolen for me, and I sighed. The one she'd grabbed meant freedom.

She was right. I couldn't stay. I needed to go. I'd promised myself forever: dance and freedom, whatever the cost.

Yeah, I didn't have time for soccer games and talking.

Grabbing my backpack from between my feet, I yanked it out with a thud and headed down the bleachers. With an exaggerated sigh—*yes, Whit, I know you think I need more boy in my life*—she followed me.

We'd been planning to go to the park, where we'd do our homework for an hour until I had to be at the studio for class. That would last an hour and a half, and then I had to run to work to cover the last two hours of my shift.

Two of four, thanks to Kesh. He'd been helping me with my weeknight shifts lately, in exchange for picking up a few of his hours on the weekends, which was fine until competition season started. Then I'd have to figure something else out.

Somehow, that's when it all clicked into place. I turned on her in the middle of the parking lot. "Vic. He's your exit strategy."

"This isn't about Vic."

"You don't want to hold me back, but you need a plan. He's your plan."

"He's not a plan. I'm crazy about him."

I snorted. "Yeah. You are that."

She put a hand on her hip. "You don't get to be an asshole about him until you at least give him a chance. You get to know him and still need to be an asshole? Fine. But the shittiest thing to do is piss on something before you even take a look at it." With her hair swinging out behind her like spears, she spun away from me back to the bleachers. The only place she knew I wouldn't follow her.

I could text her, though, and drafted a new one every break I had that night—as soon as I got to my car, once I hit the park, before dance, before work, and before bed:

Vic isn't an exit strategy. He's a mistake waiting to happen.

Think how much more fun college would be than playing house.

I can't watch you do this.

You have to pick: him or me.

HE'S TWENTY-FIVE.

I didn't send them, though, because I had to imagine how I'd respond if she were sending them to me. And that kind of reaction was not what I was going for.

Throwing myself back in bed, lights off, I flipped through my social media, unfortunately coming upon Hannah's most recent story. The picture was a selfie of her, lying in a hospital bed, and the text said, "In case anyone is wondering, there's only one person I want to ask me to Homecoming. His name starts with S and ends with an M. A++ in the middle."

She'd finished it up with endless heart emojis and round orange faces spewing kisses from themselves.

Gross. Why was I still friends with her on here?

Plugging my phone in, I stared at the ceiling. If she were my second option, I wouldn't say no. The fantasies her hair could inspire alone—I mean, you could get lost in it. Go in after a treasure hunt and decide to stay. Never come back.

I didn't have hair like that. Not many people did. Mine was light brown, indistinguishable. Thick, but pancake flat. Long, but not long enough to get lost in.

Then Sam's words came back to me: *Who I want is not going to change.*

Oh, I wanted him, too. Wanting him was not the problem.

Just to torture myself, I messaged him, **hannah had her surgery today?**

>**yeah**

it went well?<

>**easiest ever she says**

she would say that<

>bringing her flowers after school tomorrow
>she should be back wednesday

that's amazing<
just a few days for a HEART surgery<

>ablation
>more a procedure I guess

but her heart<

>yeah

bring her white flowers<

>huh

make sure they're white flowers<

>yeah?

yeah<
they're her favorite<

>hey marin

yeah<

>you're my favorite

I grinned like a complete idiot. Thank goodness my room was dark. It wasn't even original and I was over here swooning. Ridiculous.

shut up sam<
and good night<

>good night marin

Chapter 13

Either dance...

WE GOT READY FOR the dance at Hannah's—the girls in her massive bedroom and the boys in the basement.

Her mom had cheese and crackers and sparkling grape juice out on the kitchen island, along with the most recent batch of little tarts Jon had made the night before.

Up in Hannah's room, everyone cooed over Jon and how hot he was, how adorable he was with her, how he'd taken such good care of her, how he literally did everything she wanted.

She glanced over their heads at me, as if to say, *don't get too excited about it.*

My stomach tightened, but when Sam ordered everyone else into Jon and Cary's SUVs, leaving only me to ride with him, it unfurled. Maybe it was the sudden silence of the crowd locked up in a car together, or the fact that he'd taken control out of Hannah's hands, moving everyone along with such momentum and determination that she couldn't figure out how to stop it. Or maybe it was just him, and us, alone. Finally. How I wanted it.

I made sure not to look at her through the window, but she was in the front passenger seat, and Jon mostly blocked my view, anyway.

"You look fantastic," Sam muttered, his fingertips fluttering against the bared skin of my back as he helped me in the truck.

"Thanks." Hopefully that meant he appreciated the dress more than my mom did, and the waves I'd flat-ironed into my hair, the way I'd pinned it over one shoulder, not to mention the makeup Hannah had done for me, which took three times as long as when I did it, meaning it should look three times as good.

There was a pile of corsages on the seat between us, and I raised an eyebrow at him as he slipped in and slammed his door. Jon had given Hannah one inside, in front of the crowd for everyone to see. She'd accepted it, and blushed, and refused to look at me.

Twisting my way, Sam rummaged through them for a certain box, then opened it and presented it to me. Teeny, pale green bulbs sat at the base, topped with two of the most amazing flowers I'd ever seen, big multi-petal blooms colored like the plumpest peach, set around a few whisper-pink roses that matched my dress.

"It's beautiful, Sam." I reached out to touch it, but he set it in his lap to pull it out and slip it over my wrist.

He swallowed. "I know this isn't a date, but I wanted to

get you a corsage."

I glanced at the rest of them. "You got everyone a corsage."

"Only so I could give you one without you being mad at me—or without Hannah being mad at me, or without Hannah being mad at you."

"But Jon got her a corsage."

"And he didn't want it to be overshadowed by me getting everyone else one. So, they'll get them thrown on the table at dinner."

I laughed.

His smile faded. "I'm glad you like it." Turning back to the wheel, he started the truck and followed Jon's SUV as it finally pulled out of the driveway. As soon as his truck was rumbling over the pavement, his hand snuck its way to mine, one finger reaching over my pinky at first, then two.

I didn't pull away.

"Your tie matches my nails," I said. I'd only ever haphazardly mentioned how I wanted to do dark nails, a contrast with the whisper pink of my dress, but he'd been paying attention.

"I didn't think Hannah would appreciate me matching your dress."

With that, I wove the rest of my fingers through his. "You look really nice, too, Sam."

After a few turns, he asked, "Why are we eating here

again, if you don't like seafood and Cary is allergic?"

"It's Hannah's favorite. And they have good steak."

We both fell silent again, and as he helped me out of the truck at the restaurant, piling both our arms high with corsage boxes, he whispered, "On our first date, I want to take you to *your* favorite place."

Through dinner and the dance, I decided my favorite place was wherever Sam was. Even though we moved as one big group, even though I was careful to act like it wasn't a date, and even though Sam respected that, he still somehow made me feel like I was the only girl in the room. The only one he noticed at all.

After the dance, we ended up at a party in the basement of some guy Sam worked with. It was already loud and obnoxious, as if it had started hours ago, when the dance did. Hannah sat next to me on the couch, eyes closed, head resting back against the cushion.

She'd asked me to sit with her—said she needed a minute—but it almost seemed like she was asleep.

"Are you okay?" I asked, realizing she'd moved a lot

more in the last few hours than she had since she went down that night after the football game. She'd been taking it easy, but her parents had allowed her this—our last Homecoming.

"Mostly," she muttered, eyelids fluttering over to me.

"How are you feeling about Monday?" Monday was her surgery.

She shrugged. "Nervous. You know. But it's not like there's another option."

"I wish I could be there." Each patient could only have two visitors, and as she had two parents, that left me out in the cold. I asked my dad if I could stay home but he said I'd be more easily distracted if I was at school. And then I wouldn't have to catch up later.

Grabbing my hand, she smiled. "I'll be back to making ice cream cones in no time, don't you worry." But as Whitney's laugh rang out, Hannah's eyes drifted to the bar.

Whitney had been chatting with Jon and Sam for the last half hour or so. They were helping Sam's friend bartend. She laughed again and slid an arm onto Jon's bicep. Of course, never one to miss an opportunity, Jon held it out for her and flexed a few times. She laughed harder, but like he was ridiculous, not like she was pooling with desire at his feet. At least, I didn't see it that way.

But as Whitney rounded the bar and set herself between them, Hannah stood up. "Come on, let's get a drink."

"I don't think you should have a drink," I said, following

her quickly. Had her mom said anything about her drinking? Could she drink?

When Whitney noticed us, she lifted one eyebrow, and her lips curled into a smirk. "I was just congratulating these two on snagging my exes," she said. "Not an easy feat. You two are picky."

"We're not snagged," Hannah corrected, but all I could focus on was how Whitney's words were spit-laced and had the slow drawl of a serpent's hiss.

"Whit, are you drunk?" Her nickname out of my mouth was proof of my concern, but she must have not seen it that way, based on the sneer.

"Don't sound so surprised, *Mare*."

"But—" *your dad.* I wanted to say.

She laughed, short and bitter, like she knew exactly what I meant. "How about your mom? She still swallowing psycho-pharmaceuticals with her wine?"

I frowned. It had been one night. Only one. The first bottle she'd ever been prescribed and the last she'd ever filled. "She only drinks tea now." Whitney's laugh—the evil one that often called bullshit—made me cry out, "It's true!"

"That's enough," Hannah said through gritted teeth, stepping around to yank Whitney away from the boys.

"You don't get to touch me."

"You don't get to talk to Marin that way," Hannah countered.

"Why, only you can?"

"What the hell's that supposed to mean?"

"It means she's a doormat, and you're a bitch."

"Okay, okay." The boy whose house it was dropped what he was doing, since Sam and Jon were gaping holes of inaction. Putting an arm around Whitney, he walked her away. She swept her arm out as they went and knocked over whatever cups on the bar she could reach. One of them splashed purple across the counter at me. I yelped, and Whitney looked back to catch the damage: soaked into the skirt of my dress, dripping onto my thigh, slipping down my leg.

Then she was gone, up the stairs and hopefully out of the house for good.

Jon and Sam were staring at me, Jon over Hannah's head. *Yeah, you heard it right, my mom tried to kill herself when I was in third grade.* And Hannah was staring at the spot Whitney had been, not seeing anything except the spinning wheels of our past: *She's a doormat and you're a bitch.*

I loved Hannah with all of me. She was fun and charming and never defeated, all things I admired about her. But Whitney had seen inside us and what she said wasn't exactly untrue, either. Hannah did demand things. She often didn't see—or overlooked, or didn't care—what other people wanted. So, if she wasn't wrong about Hannah, did that mean she wasn't wrong about me?

A fat, fuzzy tennis ball lodged its way in my throat, and the space between my ears stretched until the pinpricks there were almost more than I could bear. Sam reached out for me, and Jon was blabbering, probably trying to pretend as if nothing had happened, but I couldn't hear him. Everything had turned to white noise.

I pushed through the crowd, a blur of color and motion, and made my way down the hall to the bathroom. Sam squeezed inside with me before I had a chance to slam the door, and I only thought one second before lifting my skirt up and into the sink. He'd seen me in a bikini.

As I held my skirt up around my waist, he turned to lock the door. "I feel like I missed something back there."

Most of the purple had rinsed out of the fabric, so I stood on my tippy toes and did my best to wring it dry. Thank goodness it was loose and flowy and not skintight. "The three of us used to be best friends. You missed all the history and witnessed the bad blood."

Sam wet a washcloth and offered it to me for my leg. As I wiped the trail off, he opened drawers until he found a blow dryer.

As he turned it on, I pulled the cord out of the wall. "Do you think I'm a doormat?"

"Of course not, Marin."

"What am I, then?"

"You're nice—gentle, thoughtful, polite."

"Kind of sounds like a doormat to me."

"How about smart and funny and laid-back? You're all those things, too."

"Laid-back, like a doormat?"

"Beautiful, with those six freckles—"

"Seven."

"Seven," he whispered. "And entrancing."

I shifted uncomfortably.

"You've always been one of my, like, twenty favorite people, but more and more lately, I try to look at other girls and just can't. Every time you tell me we're not going to happen, Jon points someone else out, but every time, I'm drawn straight back to you."

My heart beat hard, in both panic and excitement. Panic because Hannah, and excitement because it felt like all I wanted in this moment was right in front of me on a platter. All I had to do was take it.

My phone buzzed from where I'd tossed it on the counter—five quick, successive bursts. Hannah.

>**just found out**
>**you scheduled jon**
>**to spend all this time with me**
>**so you could have sam**
>**we are no longer**

I flew out of the bathroom, back through the sea of people, searching for her. Up the rickety stairs, out the kitchen door to the garage, and there—her voluptuous hair waved at me from the corner.

She was propped up on a big woodworking table, and she was... vaping? Because of something so stupid as me helping Jon along a little? Making sure someone was there for her when she was scared and I couldn't be? Making sure that someone wasn't Sam?

As I got closer, I realized, "Is that *weed*?"

Leaning forward, she hissed, "Jon says it will make me not care about anything. And I no longer want to care about you."

I batted her hand away, the one that was trying to force a vape into my mouth.

"Hannah, please. You were just saying how gross this was, remember?"

"Weed smells better than peach mango watermelon." She marveled at it in her hand. "Sort of like skunk."

"Exactly! Listen to yourself."

"You *have* always been kind of a wet blanket."

Great. A doormat and a wet blanket. Sentiments from the two best friends of my life. I pinched my fingers on the bridge of my nose to alleviate the sting, then felt a hand on my lower back. Sam.

"Where's Jon?" I asked. Did she banish him over this, too?

"He went to buy me donuts."

"What?"

"You've already forgotten that when I'm sad I need donuts?" She took a deep inhale and then exhaled directly into my face. Sam waved it away as best he could. "One night with Sam and you forget all about me?"

"It's not like that!"

"What's it like, then? Because all I can see is that you wanted Sam so much more than you wanted me that you manipulated my life to have him."

"I wanted you both! If I wanted him more than you, I wouldn't have waited so damn long!"

"Oh!" She scoffed. "That's rich, Marin. How long did you wait, huh? 'Cause as far as I can tell, it was only a few months. He's only wanted you for a couple of *months*!"

His grip on me tightened, but he didn't say anything. I would've thought that wasn't chivalrous, would've thought I wanted him to step in and stick up for me, but in that moment, I realized Hannah had handicapped me, and Sam was propping me up.

"I couldn't be there for you—I was too busy—and I knew you needed someone. That's it. I just nudged him along."

"Only so you could get what you wanted! Not because you cared about what I wanted! Or you would have sent Sam!"

"I can't control Sam, okay! I can't make him like you!"

"Play it like you're on my side, but we all know you did all this just to get him for yourself."

I stared at her. She stared at me. The air, dense with apprehension, was tactile on my exposed skin, pressing down, seeping in, suffocating. Did she think I had ulterior motives because in my situation, it's exactly why she would have done what I did? Did I have ulterior motives? Did it matter, if Sam never would have had her in the first place?

"Listen." Taking a deep breath to calm myself, I shifted on my feet. "Maybe you're a little sensitive after what Whitney said—God knows I am. But don't let her get between us."

Hannah leaned over, her hair hanging around her face so thick it made her look like a floating head. "Are you saying I'm acting like a *bitch*?"

Everyone in the garage stopped to look at her as Jon sauntered in with a fresh bag of hot donuts.

She snatched it out of his hand, and he took the vape from her. "Has she been sharing?" he asked, looking at the few people around us.

They all shook their heads.

"Oh, boy," he said. "Hannah, you need to slow down."

She wrapped her legs around him and pulled him closer, then gave me the middle finger over his shoulder.

I stepped up and shoved Jon over. "You didn't care how I felt when you started throwing yourself at him last year, but when I try to make *everyone* happy, I'm still the bad guy?"

"Last year doesn't matter, because he didn't like me," she mumbled, through both a sneer and a chunk of donut.

"And if he had, you would've walked away?" I scoffed. "Please, if he would take you now, you'd toss me aside and go for it. So don't give me this shit."

"Who are we talking about?" Jon asked.

"Nobody," Hannah snapped, but in my direction, not his. "Marin's just pissed because we're having more fun than she is."

"No," I snapped. "I'm pissed because I *am* a doormat—*your* doormat—and I'm sick of it."

We stared at each other for a long moment. It stretched into tomorrow and then arched back. Her face morphed placid. "Well, good. Because I am sick of you."

Chapter 14

...or party.

EVEN THOUGH WHIT SAID she didn't want to go to the dance, she'd bought a whole new outfit for Kesh's party, so I pulled out the form-fitting, little black dress I'd worn to my aunt's fancy wedding last summer and painted my nails a dark burgundy.

Whitney took out her lip ring and pulled her hair back. I wore black leather booties (my only pair of heels) and managed a solid—though artfully messy—fishtail braid that fell over my shoulder on one side.

We had never worked so hard. I was tired from the effort alone. But it was all worth it to have a night where things felt normal again, Vic not muscling his grotesque biceps between us.

"That's Sam's truck," I muttered, as I pulled up to Kesh's curb. It was parked right next to the open garage, like he'd been the first one here.

"Isn't that good?" Whit asked. "Don't you want in his pants?"

"I don't want in his pants," I scoffed, wanting in his pants even more when the subject was brought up.

Refusing to accept any of the implications in the look she was giving me as we got out of the car, I grabbed her hand and pulled her inside with me. Following the noise to the basement, we made our way toward Kesh, who was standing on a chair behind the bar, orchestrating something. I was so busy watching him that I walked directly into Sam.

For one awkward moment, we were nearly chest to chest, but then Kesh was jumping up and down and waving at me, so I grabbed Sam's hand and led both him and Whit over. Only, when we reached the bar, Vic was there, as if he'd been there all along, waiting for her.

I dropped Sam's hand and turned on her. "This was supposed to be our night."

She narrowed her eyes at me. "Exactly. So I thought, if you were trying to make amends, you might give him a chance."

She braced herself against him, palms on each bicep to rise on her toes and suck on his face, while I stacked the discarded plastic shot glasses scattered across the nicked wood and tried to collect myself.

Was it shitty that she'd sprung this on me, *again*?

"How old is that guy?" Sam whispered, eyes on his mustache. Gross.

"Twenty-five, supposedly."

"He probably shouldn't be at an underage party."

"Right. Someone should probably point that out to him."

He studied me but I couldn't say it. I couldn't say it to Vic, and I couldn't ask Sam to. That would be a total Hannah move. Something my mom might do. Rude and without boundary.

"Dude," Sam said, slowly looking from me to Vic as the two of them broke apart. "You lost?"

I put a hand on his arm. But for what? To stop him? Encourage him? Sam looked at me, brow furrowed ever so slightly, and I couldn't decide what message to send so I stood there, still dumbstruck, and swallowed.

They stared at us, and Sam shifted his gaze from me to them. "You look a little old for a high school party."

"He's here with me," Whit replied, but to me, as if I was the one who'd said it. She grabbed my arm and pulled herself closer to me. "Be nice! He's paranoid enough!"

"He should be!" I hissed. "You're not even eighteen. Have you told him yet?"

"Of course, I did! I'm not going to bring him to a high school party without cluing him in first. Because of you, I told him—sobbing, imagining how he'd break up with me, as disgusted as you are. But instead, it brought us closer together. Hear that? *You* brought us closer together."

I stammered, my fingers squeezing the pile of dirty plastic shot glasses so hard it hurt.

Sam cleared his throat and touched my elbow. "Wanna get out of here?"

God, yes. But that would be a date. Two of us, on our own, out in the world. I may as well have gone to the dance with him. But yes, I did want to get out of there.

Grabbing his hand—big bones and bigger knuckles, the perfect amount of rough that made you want to rub your skin along them to map the grooves, or maybe have them rub against your skin because you knew the feel of them, uniquely Sam, would yank you alive...

Ahem, not that I was noticing. Letting go, I checked back to make sure he was still following me as we left the crowd and headed down the hall that held a bedroom, an office, and at the end, a bathroom.

I picked the office.

Sam stood in the doorway. "Marin, you do know that Kesh leaves these open for people who want to..."

"Polka?"

A crack of amusement flashed on his lips.

I backed up until I could lean against the desk. "I'm not ready to sleep with you, Sam, don't worry." Kiss me silly, though—that I could use about now.

"Please, I know." He walked in and settled next to me. "You wouldn't even go to the dance with me."

"Well, that's no implication. Anyway, I thought you'd end up going with Hannah."

They would've had a lovely time, and he'd have forgotten all about me. She had to be a good kisser, with all she'd practiced on her pillow and hand back when we were in late elementary. By now, with real experience, no doubt she was the type whose kisses could annihilate a brain, turn it to mush, and demand it to follow. I mean, she could pick just about any guy in school. Why'd she have to like the one I liked?

Except, I reminded myself, I *wanted* him to like her and not me. So, it was good she'd picked him, and maybe proof she had a slice of her soul left. Maybe she was actually still in there somewhere.

"I'm not going to settle for Hannah when I want someone else," he said, examining his outstretched feet. "It doesn't make any sense."

"You two together make a lot of sense. You have the same friends. You do the same things."

He looked at me. "I get why you say that, Marin, but what matters to me is that I don't feel any connection to her. You don't always like who makes sense, you know? You like who you like."

I scowled. This was exactly the problem with Whitney and Vic. "I thought you agreed he was too old for her."

"I do." Then he smirked. "But you're not too old for me."

It was cold, even in my cropped jacket, and I didn't want to wish so badly that Sam would slip his arms between my layers and warm me up, but I did.

His hand was clutching the desk next to my hip and his pinky twitched against my thigh.

The intimacy of it, the casual ease with which he did

it, like he was so comfortable with me already, so sure... It was doing some seriously weird things to my stomach and upper respiratory cavity. Like I was on a roller coaster. Pressing, folding, flipping, flying, dropping.

His eyelashes were so close, and so long, that I imagined them catching on the finer strands of my hair, loose along my face. Or were those escaped pieces doing their job and catching him, like Imani used to say?

Studying his neckline, I opened my mouth to explain again what I was up for, what this was to me, what it had to be, but he came in quick, and his lips smothered my words. In the same way I remembered the last one, it was unlike any other *just kiss* I'd ever experienced. I'd thought that's what it could be with him—just kisses—but that first one had thrown me off my axis and this second was sizzling deep.

Screw being friends and keeping it light and fun—I wanted hot and heavy and deep. Burning lava raking heavy trails across our souls, leaving imprints in each other that no one else could reach.

No. Roadblocks and caution signs and precarious cliffs, frozen with snow and ice. I turned my head away. "This doesn't mean anything," I muttered.

"It means something to me."

Gah. And I couldn't force it out, couldn't feed him lies: *it doesn't mean anything to me.* Oh, how I wished it didn't mean anything to me.

He took my hand and shook it lightly.

I tried again. "It was only a kiss."

"You can say whatever you want, Marin, but words don't make it so. It is what it is; no matter if you say it's not."

"I could kiss any of these people here tonight and they wouldn't go home thinking it meant anything. You could kiss Hannah, and I wouldn't go home thinking it meant anything."

"You didn't drag me into that bedroom and rip my clothes off because you care about me too much, am I right?" His voice was so gentle that I kind of wanted to smack him. I didn't need gentle. *Don't be gentle with me.*

I started pacing but he stepped in my way, catching his hands on my arms. "I'm not going to let you cheapen this."

"I'm only trying to remind you what I want." The impact of it, though weak, flickered visibly across Sam's face and my stomach collapsed.

"We're past what you want. We can't help it. We just are. You can tell yourself it means nothing, but once it means something, it means something, whether you want it to or not."

I looked down at my toes, willing myself not to lean my forehead against his chest and let him envelop me. "Maybe we should go check on Whit."

He stared at me, gaze splicing into mine, forcing its way through my outer limits like he had a habit of doing. Then he dropped his hands. "Marin—"

"I don't want to talk about it, Sam. And I don't want to fight." This was why the before was always better. Before was never bitter, and before never fell apart. During and after, those were the bitter moments, and serious always fell apart. Before, though, that was the sweet spot. Imagine an endless string of befores, all with the same most favorite of persons. No time or expectations to tarnish, only heartbeats and exhilaration and stolen lips in parking lots.

We stared at each other, and not in any of the ways we had before. No, now it was a challenge. I was challenging him, he was challenging me, and he caved first. His shoulders fell and he walked to the door. The warmth of him, which I didn't know I felt until it was gone, dissipated.

"I just want easy," I tried to explain, following him.

Turning in the doorway, he replied, "Nothing about you is easy, Marin."

He stalked out of the room, down the hall back to the bar, leaving me in the doorway to work up an even pissier mood than the one Whit and Vic had put me in. If that's what kissing Sam was going to do to me, then hell if I'd kiss him again.

Storming through the incoming crowd of Sam's friends, fresh from the dance in fancy suits and dresses, shiny ties and high heels, pink collar stains and freshly applied lipstick, I worked my way against them, a struggling fish going upstream. Up the stairs and to the garage, I stopped at the first person I saw with a vape and sat down on a pail. Unfortunately, this nondescript, skinny dude seemed to think I'd invited him into my life as soon as he shared it with me. He kept up with the lame conversation, flipping his lustrous Hannah-colored hair back off his forehead on a super-regular basis until I could stand it no more.

"What do you want from me?" I asked, finally looking at him.

"I, um, I want, um, nothing, really," he stammered.

"Like, do you want someone to chat with, are you hoping to get my number, do you want to make out or think I might sleep with you? What is it?"

"I... I was hoping to get your number."

"I don't give out my number. And we will not happen."

"Yeah, okay." Like girls were bitches to him all the time.

He *was* sort of cute, and those doe eyes tugged at the little bit of guilt I allowed harbor inside me. I'd been harsh, and anyway, Sam needed to understand we weren't something.

"Tonight, okay? Only tonight. But no heavy petting." Standing, I pushed him up against the tool corkboard and placed my lips on his. Mechanical, technical, precise.

He was willing, very. Weren't they all? My disgust with proving my mom right on the male species was flooded out by the disgust I felt for myself. And his kisses, which were wet and squirmy, lips made of earthworms, were definitely not up to the standard I had recently become accustomed to.

But I would stay here and kiss him until Sam heard my

message. In action, and not just in word. If I knew him at all, he'd be coming to find me sooner or later. But it was Whit who interrupted us first.

"Let's go," she said, dragging me off. "You're in trouble."

"With Sam, right? He saw me?"

"Yes," she said, as we got in my car. "When you didn't come back, he went to find you. I didn't know what he was so worked up about until *I* found you, but he was back in a second, and *ooo* boy. Kesh went to pour him a shot, but he took the bottle and finished it."

I looked at her, eyes wide.

"There wasn't much, but still. He was *not* happy."

I pounded the back of my head against the headrest.

"That's what you wanted, right?" she asked, tart.

From the passenger side, she reached over to turn the keys in my ignition and pointed to the clock. Of course, because everything unraveled when you got this deep into the night.

She'd normally close her door now, and I'd drive us home. Then, in the morning, everything would be reset. But I wasn't sure how I could reset all this. With Sam. With her. My instincts were no good anymore.

The door was splayed wide open, and she sank into the seat, resting her head back and turning her head to the house. "Sam is perfect. He would be so good to you, and you won't even let yourself have him."

Won't. Not can't, but won't. Like nothing was stopping

me but myself.

Only, watching her story from the outside, she wasn't stopping herself and she should've been. So, who was right, when clearly she was wrong?

"Go home, Marin." She set a foot on the curb. "And call Sam in the morning when he's not drunk. Apologize."

"Wait." I caught her arm as she ducked to get out. She twisted back to me. "I will if you get rid of Vic. Or I won't, if you want me single if you're single. I'll literally do whatever you want if you cut him off."

"There's nothing you can do, Marin. It's not your choice, and I'm not under your control. We dumped Hannah for a reason, remember? I can't believe…" She shook her head and scoffed. "This is literally how I'd imagine her acting in this situation, you know?"

"That's not fair."

"Maybe not, but it's true."

My emotions churned, so many of them from so many corners of this night, that I couldn't tell what was what anymore, only that I was overwhelmed with them, too many and too much. Even in that, though, I did know what was true. And what was important.

"Me or him, Whit."

Her face went still and unreadable, a twitch of a cheek locking into place. No strain, no anger, no emotion at all. It reminded me of how it felt, compiling my insides in the face of my mother. And for that one second, I thought I'd maybe gotten this wrong.

But no. A twenty-five-year-old with a seventeen-year-old had predator written all over it. How could that end with her not being taken advantage of, one way or the other?

I'd expected her to tear up at the thought of losing me, come to her senses and all that. But she said nothing. She got out of the car and slammed the door, walked to the house, and disappeared inside.

Should I go in after her? Maybe she was breaking up with him right now. We were everything to each other, always had been. But then I'd have to face Sam, drunk and confused and angry with me.

Resting my fingertips on the clock, I reminded myself how everything could so easily go wrong late at night—it was a foregone conclusion, really—so I went home to deal with it all in the more accurate light of morning.

Chapter 15
Either lies...

I WOKE UP THE next morning, guilt thick as mucus pressing heavy on my chest, stuffing up my nose, clogging my ears, crusty on my eyes. It didn't matter that I didn't feel like I'd done anything wrong. It mattered that I *had* done the thing that Hannah was now holding against me.

Rolling over, I checked my phone. Things were always better in the morning, and surely Hannah would've texted me the moment she woke up, but all I found were a million tags—people attaching me to pictures from the night before. No texts, no messages. Nothing from Sam, either, which wasn't much of a surprise, I guess. After fighting with Hannah, I'd asked him to take me home, then choked on tears the whole way and gave him a scrambled "thank you" before nearly tripping out of his truck.

The pictures looked good, though. One Jon had taken at the restaurant, all ten of us beaming. Hannah and me in front of Sam's truck, arms thrown around each other. One I'd posted at the dance of Hannah and Jon slow-dancing.

Did she know how easy it would be to make me believe

I'd manipulated her life for my own gain? Did she realize how easily I fell into other people's reality, letting their feelings and perceptions overtake mine?

Staring at my trophy shelf—old awards from our childhood dance studio and new ones from high school competitions—I willed myself to focus on what I believed I'd done. I hadn't hurt anyone. I hadn't pushed anyone. Jon was willing and waiting for access, which was all I'd given him. She hadn't complained when she was eating his tarts and cakes and they were spending hours watching reality TV when I couldn't be there.

But those trophies, like everything else in my room and my life—the clothes, the makeup, the books, the music downloaded on my phone—it was all attached to Hannah. She'd helped me paint my room gray after my mom left. Hunted for the throw pillows and bean bag and rug. Gifted me every bit of color accent that made it in the room to stay. Surprised me with an obscene amount of fairy lights on my sixteenth birthday. Every dance poster and figurine I had, she'd found shopping with her mom, since my dad never took me shopping and my mom refused to help me decorate the bedroom in the house she'd left behind.

Hannah thought of me, all the time. And now, when it counted most, I had only been thinking of myself. That's how she felt. And even if that wasn't how I saw it, I couldn't let my best friend sit in that without doing anything to change it.

you up? I texted. **can I come over?**

Rolling over and burrowing back into the covers, I set my phone on the pillow next to my face, then closed my eyes and willed it to buzz back a response.

When the silence got too loud and obnoxious for me to bear, I took a shower to pass the time. Time did feel like it went faster in there, clicking away as fast as the water pounded on me. This was what my mom said she missed most about her life with my dad: the water pressure.

Standing under it until my skin was bright red and the steam was smoking up the mirror, I slipped back to my room for jeans, my favorite tee, and my coziest sweater, then checked my cell again.

Nothing.

I tried calling.

And calling.

And calling.

My dad was in the kitchen when I came down, coffee and slippers and big hands fumbling through the news on his phone. "Morning, kid. How was the dance?"

"Miserable." I slid into the chair across from him with yogurt and a spoon.

He looked up.

"Yeah," I confirmed. "Hannah and I got in a huge fight."

"Want me to make you some cinnamon rolls?"

I held up my yogurt, though I knew he was offering because he thought the smell would make me feel better.

And it might, but I didn't deserve cinnamon rolls.

"She's not speaking to me," I muttered as he went back to his phone.

He looked up again. "Want to go out for breakfast and talk about it?"

I imagined how this might play out, me talking and him looking uncomfortable. Advice for boys and betrayal and missed kisses were not in his toolbox. "No, I want to fix it."

"Then go fix it."

I nodded. Finished my yogurt. Dropped the container and spoon in the sink. Grabbed my keys and the clutch that still had my wallet and lip gloss in it. Went for my car. Blasted the radio so I couldn't think and made my way through the three expansive neighborhoods between us. Up, up, up her long driveway.

It wasn't as easy to get out of the car, though. I waited, wondering if she'd come bounding out like she usually did. Even when she wasn't expecting me, the plantation shutters on her window would flicker and she'd be down in a flash. Her shutters, though, were closed and flat—they may as well have been boarded up.

The wind pressed against the car as it whipped through and around the trees, shaking them free of the dead leaves still clinging there, raining them down and scattering them across the drive. The oaks in her yard always did that, kept some dead leaves through the season until the buds began to grow fresh.

Clutching, desperate to stay attached.

My stomach, heavy with rocks, anchored me to the seat. But I needed to know, and I needed to get it over with.

Thirty-two steps to her door. Three breaths to ready myself. Two knocks.

Maybe a doorbell for good measure.

Twenty-three excruciating seconds of me trying not to look through the windows to check if someone was coming before it swung open on her mom, dressed in business casual on this lazy Sunday morning. Her hair, as voluptuous as Hannah's, was tamed back in a bun.

"Hi, hon!" she cried, making no move to let me in like she normally would.

"Is Hannah home?" I asked.

"Nope." But she didn't say she'd let her know I'd stopped by, like she usually did.

Where would she be right now? I checked my phone. It was only ten. She didn't have a job, didn't volunteer, didn't have anywhere to be. "Really?" I asked.

"You should have a coat on, Marin. The temperature is going to keep dropping today. Big storm coming in tonight." Mrs. Watson was obsessed with the weather channel, and her weather app, and the radar option in her weather app. She'd grown up in tornado alley, so we forgave her this incessant need to discuss and analyze the climate.

But the big storm was happening right now. A tornado

of regret and sorrow and desperation swirling around my feet, lifting my hair, pressing in on all sides of me. "Snow?"

"Ice, hail."

Desperation for what, I wasn't sure. To turn back time, to talk to Hannah, to make things right. I couldn't be the reason things had gone wrong. Anything but it being my fault. Anything to avoid the guilt always swimming like a shark in my gut, waiting for the smallest drop of blood. Especially on the eve of her surgery. "She's really not here?"

"Sorry, honey." But she looked at me so sad, like I'd lost something.

Which made me only more certain she was there. Unless... "She's not at the hospital already, is she? Did she have another arrythmia?"

"Already?" Mrs. Watson's brow furrowed, her perfectly applied and undoubtedly expensive foundation moving smoothly with it. "Her ablation was weeks ago. Why would she have another arrythmia?"

"She had her ablation surgery weeks ago?" I echoed. "Doesn't she go in tomorrow?"

Mrs. Watson relaxed—her limbs, her face, her thoughts. "Tomorrow is her wisdom teeth. Her heart is tip-top. All fixed."

"All fixed?" *Weeks ago?*

"Well, she wasn't eating well, you know, with the stress of it, so we're still working on the anemia, but her extra passage is burned away. All gone."

Cold. I felt cold. But the numb kind, fingers tingling and rocks sinking. Wrapping my sweater tighter around me, I asked, "When? When did she have heart surgery?"

"I don't know, a month ago? That week right after she collapsed at the game."

No. It wasn't cold. It was utter stillness. Absence, vacancy, the eye of the storm. I was in the center of my world crashing down.

"She probably didn't want to worry you. It was a simple procedure. They put a lead in her groin, didn't even need to sedate her. Done within an hour."

But she *did* want to worry me. She had. "They didn't need to...go in through her chest?"

"They never planned on it, hon."

I stumbled back, almost falling off the steps.

But why would she lie to me? Just because she didn't want me with Sam?

Her face appeared next to her mom's. Mirror images, but one confused and the other panicked. I had only seen her panicked once before. The day she got on stage for her first solo, back when we were doing competitions. No one understood it, she'd always ached to be the star, but she told me after—only me—that it was the being alone she hadn't been able to bear.

She was terrified of being alone. I knew that. But even if I'd taken Sam, I would never have left her alone. How could she have thought I would? And she was mad at *me* for manipulating *her* life? What about my emotions—the fear and agony and turmoil of thinking they had to crack her chest open, that her heart was weak...

Who would do that to another person?

Tears sprung to my eyes, turning to chips of ice before they could make it out, the crystals obscuring her face, which swam through the bent light before me. Spinning, I tore to my car. I had to get away.

Hearing Hannah's footsteps scrambling down the steps, I moved faster, flying on the gusts of wind that were swirling around me and slamming the door before she could catch up.

"Marin! Wait!"

Keys in the ignition. Car, started.

"I'm sorry, I didn't mean to scare you! You're right! It was stupid, I don't know what I was thinking! I just didn't want to lose you! Please!"

Didn't want to lose me, or didn't want to lose Sam? I met her eyes, a molten metal, and hoped mine were hard and unforgiving. Then I backed out, not caring the slightest that she was chasing me barefoot down the drive.

At least it was obvious to both of us now, what had happened and who had done it. At least it was clear. A clean cut. And I was free.

But freedom, come to find out, felt like breaking into pieces. Shorn, splintered bits falling to the pit of my stomach like a soft rain. Quicksand sucking the past away.

I had to pull over and breathe. Forget. Remember. All the times she'd lied about this and that and who knows what else to get what she wanted. The daring and laughter and ice cream cones as big as her hair. The security of being a best friend.

Gone, with a pop. A pinprick. That's what it felt like. Then the aftermath flooded in and crashed against all the *me* she'd helped build. That part of me was now washed away. Gone. Lost.

What was I supposed to be doing? Oh, yeah. I'd texted Sam, asked where he was, if he had a minute. He was at work—meet him behind the grocery store, he'd said. *You'll see my truck back there.*

Because he was my next best friend. Because he was the one I should've been apologizing to. Because I was free. All of it tumbled around in my chest as I drove the rest of the way there. Freedom felt like loss, but it also felt like hope.

He was sitting on a cement platform, leaning forward with his hands curled around the edge, his arms straight and elbows locked. Waiting for me.

Hannah never waited for me. I just had to keep up.

Swinging the door open so fast and wide it almost hit his truck, I got out and strode to him.

"Hey," he said, hopping down to ground level. "I'm only on break but could take my lunch if you need me to."

I stopped in front of him. Wanted to lean against him

and cry.

I would not cry. That's not what I was here for.

Stepping into him, I tipped my face up, closing my eyes as my lips landed on his. Real lips, real kisses, real hands sliding around my waist, a thud on the ground—one of our phones, but neither of us cared. He met my frenzied pace and then guided me down, brought me to a place where I could feel the emotion in the kiss, the words he'd said and the ones he hadn't, the choices I should have made and the intent that had laced the air clean around us for months.

Months sped up to meet us, months of me making the wrong choice, listening to the wrong person. Months in one kiss was a lot to take in, especially when I was off-axis in the first place.

Pulling back when it started to hurt too much, I looked down to find the tips of our toes attached. My chest was heaving, and all the loose tendrils of me, swaying in the wind since they'd been disconnected from Hannah, were linking up to Sam, in so many places and in so many ways.

He put a hand to my face and lifted my gaze to his, looked me in the eye and made me face it. Not that I could imagine a moment when I wouldn't want to face him, and us, and what we could be. It was all the time wasted that was hard to look at.

"I thought last night I might've lost you for good," he said.

I shook my head, but the wind shook my hair harder. "I'm sorry about that, and about the last few months. It wasn't fair, and I should've..." The 'should-haves' got caught in my throat, though—the admission that I picked a shitty best friend over a great guy, that I was too stupid to see them both clearly, that I had put him second, as a person, and what a grave mistake it had been.

"Don't beat yourself up for my sake," he said. "Never for my sake, okay?"

Right. This was how it was supposed to feel.

"I have no complaints," he muttered.

I leaned into him and he pressed his palm to my back, like *yes, stay here, on me, with me, by me.* Or maybe, *yes, I feel it, too.* The tug, the riptide, the current, the sweeping glitter of a shooting star, dragging us down, dragging us under, carrying us along, burning us bright.

My chest folded in on itself, a million times in quick succession, like an illusion collapsing into reality. He was a reality. I wrapped my arms around him as the pressure in my chest unfolded, opening up to accept this something new, and we clung to each other until he had to get back to work.

Chapter 16

...or truth.

I WOKE UP THE next morning, regret thick as mucus pressing heavy on my chest, stuffing up my nose, clogging my ears, crusty on my eyes. It didn't matter that I hadn't done anything wrong. It mattered that Whit might very well have picked Vic last night. And if she did, it was because I pushed her to choose.

I rolled over for my phone and texted her: **you up? can I come over before work?**

I really didn't have much time, so I showered, then checked my phone again. Dressed, checked it. Foundation and mascara, checked it. Blow-dried my hair, checked it.

whit?<

Socks and shoes, checked it. Made sure I had everything in my purse, checked it. Stood in the kitchen and ate a bagel at the counter, the entire time watching it.

My dad padded into the kitchen, face blurry with sleep. With a nod, he shuffled over to the coffee pot as my mom clattered in from the garage. She dropped her gym bag just inside the door, hung her keys on their hook, tucked her water bottle under her arm, set the yoga mat against the wall, and sighed.

"Mornin'." My dad nodded. "Want some coffee?"

She tried not to drink coffee, caffeine and all, but today she looked at him and nodded.

"Thanks for starting it before you left," he said, turning to get her a cup. Then, "Marin's worried about something."

I turned in surprise.

"She hasn't spoken yet, just keeps chewing on her lip."

"What is it?" my mom asked me, taking the coffee from my dad and sitting at the table.

"Nothing. I just—I gave Whit an ultimatum last night, and now she's not answering my texts."

My dad whistled and my mom raised a brow.

"What?"

"Ultimatums are never a good idea." My dad joined my mom at the table. They sat next to each other but feet apart, against the far wall.

"They've never worked for me," my mom admitted, sly glance toward my father.

I checked my phone one last time, and in the face of Whit's silence, spun on my heel to go find her.

But what would I say? I'm not sorry? You're being stupid? I'm just trying to save you?

Ugh. That's what we'd hated about Hannah. Her always

trying to save us from ourselves, even when it was stupid things, preferences. Her opinions were always better, and she couldn't see past them to accept that we might disagree.

It'd been exhausting, and we'd hated it.

I'd have to go with I'm sorry. I was being stupid. Anything to save us, you and me.

And as soon as those thoughts hit my brain, I knew what that anything was. It was giving him an actual chance, which I'd said I'd do and didn't.

I pressed my ear to Whitney's front door before ringing the bell, so I'd know what I was getting into, but all was quiet.

Miri answered—Whit's body double but with freckles. "Hey, Mare, what's up?"

"Whit home?"

She laughed. "No, pretty sure she doesn't live here anymore."

"What?"

"Yeah, moved her entire room out last week."

"*What?*"

"She didn't tell you?" Her eyebrows furrowed. "Come see if you want." Leaving the door open, she headed to the bedrooms, expecting me to follow. I wasn't thinking, because *what?* But my feet moved anyway.

We wedged in the doorway together, looking into the abandoned space. Her desk was even gone. *Her desk.* She'd moved furniture. The closet door was flung open, only a handful of items still hanging, and the floor was bare. She'd had such a pile on the floor of that closet. The bed was naked—no pillows, no blanket—and her end table was empty, too, the drawer gaping open as if to emphasize that no one lived here anymore.

I couldn't speak. I wanted to yell. How long had she been lying to me about him? How long had she kept it all a secret? And why? Was I that awful? That judgmental?

Me or him.

Okay, fine, but this was about more than friendship or love, this was about illegal relationships and men taking advantage and how twisted must he be? It was out of hand, and at least I wasn't a *liar*.

Suddenly, Whit was a liar.

Biting my lip and holding my throat, I was able to compose myself enough to get Vic's address and get out of there.

Sliding into my car, I typed furiously:

stopped by your house<

saw your room<

cannot believe you've been lying to me<

or that you picked a 25yo over your best friend<

who even are you anymore<

Playing with the paper Miri had written his address on,

I waited. I didn't really have time to go there before work, but if she begged me…

Or she'd keep ignoring me, as she had been all morning. Obviously, she was waiting for an apology, but I didn't think I could go there now. I might have bluntly and insensitively expressed concern, but she'd been lying. *To me.*

I could barely comprehend it. We were each other's truth. When everyone else was full up on bullshit, we'd been there for each other. And we'd dealt each other harsh realities before but had always stayed to help pick each other back up. Did she really think she wouldn't need to be picked back up after this? Could she really believe she was safe with a twenty-five-year-old?

Nearly shaking, I drove to work and parked one over from my usual spot. Sam was there, always early, but he wasn't waiting for me.

Right. Of course. He shouldn't be waiting for me. He should be sprinting in the other direction. That's what I'd wanted, right?

I exhaled hard as I slammed my car door against the winter wind and made my way across the lot. Garbage swirled around my feet, bits of paper freed from the dumpster and coupons dropped by customers.

Bracing myself to see him, to face him, this guy I'd never wanted to hurt—*what had I been thinking, I should never have kissed him in the first place, I knew better*—I yanked on the door, spine rigid and limbs locked.

But the storeroom was empty, steel shelving stacked high and foreboding. The back of a grocery store would make a good haunted house: tall and dark, shadows and shapes looming over your shoulder everywhere you turned. The creak of the baler that pressed boxes into cubed bales of cardboard, the blood and gore that could come of that. I shivered as the door shut behind me, sealing out the cold but closing in the darkness.

The echo of the ancient time clock as I punched in, the shuffle of footsteps—I jerked my head in that direction, but it was only Kesh down at the other end, pulling a few boxes of cereal off the steel to go stock. He waved as our manager, words spitting out almost on top of one another, swept into the back room with Sam on his heels.

Sam.

His eyes were droopy and dark, his hair a tousled mess, his tie off-center. I wasn't sure he'd ever looked better. Vulnerable and honest, real and raw, like he'd just laid it all on the stage, everything he was and everything he wanted to be. Not that he acknowledged me. Not even with a glance.

Of course not. This was how it felt to get what you wanted sometimes.

Our manager was instructing Sam to switch out three of the end caps, which would no doubt take his entire eight-hour shift.

"I could help," I offered. But *why?*

Because it made him look at me.

Stepping back, I bit down on my lip and shook my head. Our manager was spitting out plans for how he'd shaped the day, how I was needed at the service desk, how one of the cashiers had called in, so no stocking for me today. I somehow caught it, even though all I could hear, really, was Sam's eyes on me.

They were disappointed and desensitized. Hard and clean like a one-way mirror, showing me only my reflection. No more intent, interested, curious rakes through my soul. No, now I was a ghost.

To both of them. Had I lost both of them?

"Marin," our manager said. "Did you hear me?"

"I'm sorry." I extricated myself from the prison that I'd put myself in and yanked my inaudible but surely visible pleas from Sam to look at my boss. "You needed me up front an hour ago."

"Yes, so can we make it quick?"

"Of course. Sorry." Sam was gone now anyway, drifting away on an iceberg down to Kesh.

Maybe I should be grateful that I'd be stuck up front all day. It would give us some space, even though the space I already felt was gaping. Awful.

What was wrong with me?

The service desk was pretty slow, usually, so I spent most of the first half of my shift trying to craft a text to Sam, something along the lines of 'I'm sorry. Please, I want us to be friends. We're so good as friends.' But then my fingers would keep going. 'Don't leave me like this. Come back.'

And I'd be so furious with myself, I'd delete the whole thing.

When I was released for break, I snuck down the bread aisle, past the piles of shiny produce, and into the dark shadows of the back room to the time clock.

Regret was standing behind me, leaning over my shoulder, whispering all the things I'd done wrong in my ear. With Sam, with Whit, last night and before.

Gah, *before*. Even before was letting me down.

Misery tugged at me, pulled me under, swam through my head, oozed out the fractures in my chest. In and out and in and out and around again, too thin to catch.

Was this what depression felt like? Like you wanted to swallow yourself to make the deadened ends go away? Like you were waiting for a rebirth that might never come? Or was this just how it felt when you hurt someone you cared about?

"Why'd you do it?" Sam asked, his voice coming out of nowhere. And then the rest of the bustle filled in behind him. The door that he'd come through swinging shut, the chatter from the store, the whir of the freezer, the pop and shove from the heavy sealed door as one of the assistant managers came out from restocking milk. The strong smell of frozen crystals clinging to frosted metal hung in the air for a moment as she stripped the community jacket off, hung it on a hook, and worked her way down to the baler with some boxes. Hoisting them in, she closed the cage with a clang and pressed the button to flatten them.

Sam stopped waiting for my answer and headed downstairs to the dungeon break room. Did he want me to follow? I mean, I don't know why else he'd go down there, so I did. What else would I do with regret and misery poking and prodding at me?

My mouth was dry. My tongue coated with powder. Could I even speak? What could I say?

Last night it had made so much sense. I'd even explained it to him in Kesh's basement office. *I could kiss someone tonight and it wouldn't mean anything.* So why did it feel like it meant something? Why did it feel like I'd ruined something if there'd been nothing to ruin? Unless he was right. Unless we were what we were, no matter what I said about it.

Narrow, shallow steps. Rough cement walls. Darker and damper, with exposed wires and pipes. Hanging fluorescent lights, only half of which worked, all of which seemed to flicker. Drifting spiderwebs dropping from the chains that held the lights in place. This level was for the brave ones, the ones who could handle a basic haunted house without flinching.

I used to be one of those people. The unflinchable.

But as Sam shoved into a brighter, finished room, I flinched.

"Did they remodel?" I asked, looking around at the not-rusty sink and the freshly painted floor. "Did they *wallpaper*?" Which made sense, since the paint had stained from the age before, when smoking inside was normal.

I ran my hand along the table, a new oak oval with matching chairs instead of the two rickety card tables you had to prop up with your knee if you didn't want your soda sliding over to the next person. And the folding chairs that pinched your back if you tried to get comfy.

"Why'd you do it?" he asked again, turning on me in the middle of the space and running a hand over his head. He cradled the back of his neck in his palm as if something hurt.

I backed into the counter and held onto the sink. "I thought I made that perfectly clear at the party." But clear as I'd like to be, I was shaking. When had I started shaking? Did I have a fever?

He paced, back and forth. It looked downright crazy in the small space. "I didn't think, in all this, that you'd pick some other guy." But he was talking to himself, mumbling to the floor, like he was working out a complicated calculus problem.

"I didn't pick anyone. A kiss doesn't mean anything."

He stopped. "That's why? To prove it didn't mean any-thing between us?"

Either I was brilliant for guessing this would happen if I got too close to him or I was an idiot who did idiot things and I owed him an apology. "I'm sorry," I decided. "I never wanted to hurt you. Please know that, if nothing else."

"I can't do this anymore."

What should have been relief knit a complicated knot of pressure in my throat, but I could accept this fate. It had been the inevitable culmination I'd been waiting for. I nodded. Submission.

He looked steadily back.

Hung moments on puppet strings. Fat, wide hooks, dropping down from the tangle of wires hidden above the drop ceiling, to catch time. One missed and snagged the sharp corner of my heart, and another went off-center and gutted me. Closing my eyes, I pictured the stuck hook: thick and bronze, rusty. Running my hands down my abdomen, I pushed it down and out, then held the wound to catch the blood.

Opening my eyes, I was almost surprised to see that my hands were clean and there was no gaping hole in my stomach, no nick in my chest.

Sam moved forward. I looked at my feet so I didn't have to see him up close as he squeezed between the chairs and my body, glued in place at the sink, to get to the door. So I didn't have to see him leave.

Only, his shoes ended up in front of me, his head dipped to reach my lips, and his mouth coaxed mine up-up-up.

I responded because that's what you do when someone puts their lips on yours, but it took me a bit to fall into what was happening. And just as I registered fully the warmth that was Sam Hanson, as I crossed the point of no return and kissed him back with a strong sort of purpose, as I reached out to catch one of those hooks, to yank it hard and stop time for good, as I let go of the sink behind me and moved to gather him up because it was all I wanted, even if it was a last time, right then, before I could link myself around him, he pulled away.

"This is it, Marin," he whispered, having caught my arms with his hands. He tucked them back at my sides and explained, "You're in or I'm out." Then he spun and shoved his way back into the haunted house.

I leaned there, propped against the counter, trying to catch my breath and trying to hold on to everything I thought had made sense.

Every pair of steps I took thereafter sounded like *you're in or I'm out. You're in or I'm out, you're in or I'm out, you're in or I'm out.* Up the stairs, across the store, back to the service desk. *You're in or I'm out.*

I practically ran to the time clock when I was finished with my shift, slowing my feet as I made my way to the loading dock.

They were already outside, Sam and Kesh. But Sam was standing down on the parking lot like he was leaving instead of sitting next to Kesh, who was rapidly downing a bag of powdered donut balls.

Kesh lifted the sleeve, offering me one. "I have no alcohol, so Sam is leaving us."

"You're leaving?" I squeaked, my attention darting to him in panic. It was hard enough, reining in the loose and unhinged emotions that were bouncing from my gut to my chest to my head to my gut, without having to worry he'd changed his mind.

"Hopefully with you," he said softly. As if the kiss in the break room had cleared out all the crap from last night and we were righted again, the two of us, friends plus whatever more.

It further enforced my decision, because how could I lose that again, when I might be losing Whitney? I'd hardly been able to breathe when I thought I'd lost both of them.

I took the few steps to the edge of the cement, my toes hanging off the cliff I was about to jump. "I'm in," I whispered. "Of course I'm in."

Sam's smile lit the darkness and Kesh's chuckle drifted on the wind behind me. "You know, how about I get out of here, huh?"

Sam and I ignored him, staring at each other as he left. Once it was silent and heavy again, Sam grinned through that intense gaze of his that no longer felt like spiders but feathers.

Feathers, what lovely things: soft and downy, whisper-light, providing warmth and protection, stimulating at the point of contact.

He offered me his hand and, slipping my fingers through

his, I laced them like sneakers, tight and intertwined. He led me to his truck. Now that I thought about it, it was kind of freezing. Somehow, it even smelled cold. Bare and abandoned, like earth and light had been sucked dry through a straw to the heavens.

Sam's truck, on the other hand, smelled like him, like earth and light. He turned the ignition and blasted the heat, set the radio on low, and began flipping maniacally through the stations.

I turned off the music, not wanting anything to distract me. I wanted to remember this: the jump.

"That guy last night," I started. "He honestly meant nothing. He was the worst. I mean, even if he'd been the best, he still wouldn't have meant—" I stopped as he settled a heavy gaze on me.

"I know," he muttered, his voice dropping raw and husky. "I knew. I should've known. Whatever, it doesn't matter. Because this?" Holding my hands in his, he leaned forward. "This one is going to mean something. So much that not even you will be able to deny it."

His hands rose to my face, and when his lips touched down, it felt like he was drinking me in, a contrast to our first kiss when it had been me feeding off him, in control and directing traffic. Not being in control felt like a snowball careening down a hill, gaining momentum and unable to stop. Snowballs often crashed into powder and dust at the bottom of an avalanche.

Avalanches were a disaster.

I gasped, unable to breathe with the heaviness of it all, and pulled back. "What if I screw up again? What if I don't mean to and I do anyway?" I didn't just mean him and me. I meant Whit, and life. I meant everything.

His gaze laid me bare. "I have faith in you, and in us." Which was almost like answering the question he didn't know I'd asked.

Faith and hope seemed to be working with him, but they weren't what I'd been using on Whit. She probably could have used a little faith and hope. Not that it mattered anymore, now that I knew she'd been lying to me possibly all our lives.

I stared out the windshield, at the wind whipping the world around. It sounded like my dad whispering in my ear. *Hope*, he was saying, loudly. *Choose the hope.* And here was Sam in front of me with faith enough for both of us.

Taking my hands from his, I wrapped them around his neck, letting my palms slide over his hair—softer than it looked—and kissed him back.

Like it meant something.

Chapter 17

Either past...

I WAS FINISHING OFF the last half hour of my volunteer shift at the shelter when Whitney pushed through the revolving door. Her hair, back to its normal color, was blown out smooth, and she wasn't wearing any makeup. The lip ring was gone, and she wore a sweater with jeans and black boots. It was the most polished I'd seen her since Hannah had anything to say about it.

She stopped when she saw me and looked back at the doors she'd come through, as if I was enough to make her turn around. And though decisive with her next step forward, her shoulders slouched, sinking her from almost six feet to a collapsible paper doll.

Did I do that to her? I'd always thought it was Hannah.

"I'm here for an application," she said.

"An application?" I repeated. We had applications for a million things—requesting shelter, help to escape domestic abuse, drug and alcohol support, counseling, rehab pamphlets, the list went on.

"I want to work for the suicide hotline."

"Oh. Sure." Rummaging through the haphazard stacks on the shelf behind the desk, I said, "I thought you were going to be a lawyer."

"I thought you were going to be a dancer."

"When I was ten, maybe."

"Exactly," she clipped, making the small expanse of desk between us seem large and foreboding, a world of hurt skittering across it between us.

Finding the right packet, I handed it to her, trying to figure out how to start over. I didn't want it to be like that. I'd never wanted it to be like that. So, I ignored her attitude, which I used to do on a fairly regular basis when we were friends. "And now?"

"Now I'm more interested in helping people." She looked down and grabbed a pen from the canister of plastic flowers.

"That's not new, though. You always liked helping people."

She glanced up at me, and I could see it in her eyes, the same scene playing out in both our minds—the first time she realized she could give her birthday gift cards to the homeless man we often saw sifting through garbage at the park. After that, we'd both asked for Sub Stop and Shopmart cards instead of the clothing stores Hannah always put on her list.

"How are your parents? How's Miri?" I asked. "Your dad still make his Chex mix?"

"Of course. I had to go with him to the grocery store last week because he needed someone to push a second cart of supplies." She rolled her eyes, and I laughed. Chex-mix season was really the only time we'd chosen Whitney's. We'd sit at the kitchen table playing multiple-person solitaire with her mom and sister, Christmas music in the background, while waiting for fresh batches to be laid out to dry. Like a warm cookie, it was so much better than the final, room-temperature product. "So, if not a dancer, then what?" she asked.

"Physical therapy." Her loopy writing yanked me back to the days I'd look over her shoulder as she filled out our summer bucket list. "Where are you going to school?"

"UMKC." She didn't look up as she printed her address on the second line. "Just part time. While I work. You?"

"Wash U, hopefully." It felt like everyone had heard back from their schools already, and that was making me itchy.

"You and Hannah rooming together and joining a sorority and timing your pregnancies to coincide?"

"Hannah's going to KU."

Whit looked up. Raised an eyebrow.

"We sort of...broke up."

She smirked. "Good for you."

Good for me? All these years I'd figured it had been us who'd dropped her, when maybe she'd called Hannah on her bullshit that long ago and I'd totally missed it.

Sam's voice floated down the hallway from behind me.

He was walking in step with Jack, the weekend manager, and explaining how he'd left the stockroom for whoever was coming in next.

Jack slid into the desk chair and nodded at Whitney.

"She's filling out an application," I explained. "Suicide hotline."

"Does she have any training?" he asked, looking at her.

"I don't know, but she'd be great at it," I replied. Whitney's head tilted up, wheat shafts spilling aside, and she looked at me.

"She a friend of yours?" he asked.

This question seemed to pause the otherwise relatively speedy nature of time, as our past rushed up to meet us, tangible in the air—a drawn, taut moment, during which memories sped through my mind like a flip book.

"Yes," I replied, at the same time Whitney said, "Would it help me get the job?"

"It would," he replied, staring her down with the kind of leveling gaze she was actually quite good at herself, if I remembered correctly.

She nodded at him, then looked at me. "Thanks."

Nodding, I slid past Sam to leave. I should've been excited that it was Sunday, that he'd taken the day off, that we were going to spend it together, but instead I was thinking about freedom and college and how seeing Whitney's handwriting could so quickly bring me back to the days we'd first discovered the drugstore. A month after my mom had ended up in the hospital, we'd ridden our bikes to check it out, this place she'd gotten the medication that had made her sick. But it had only been magical, even then. Hannah's first attempt at a six-inch ice cream cone had fallen splat on the floor, and our friendly neighborhood pharmacist had appeared in a nanosecond with napkins and a mop, filling up three more cones so my lip would stop trembling.

Not that it was the fallen ice cream causing it, of course. Unfortunately, his kindness made me burst into tears, and the library's front lawn—its circular stone bench around the old oak tree—had collected me when I'd come out weeping. Hannah had sat on the bench and licked through all three cones while Whit and I had lain in the freshly mown grass, our feet stuck under Hannah and our gaze beyond the branches.

I could still feel the bruised tips of the grass leaking onto my fingers, could still see the shorn bits thrown sideways and about. Plus, that smell...

Sam slung my scarf around my neck, looping me back to the present, and led me across the lot to his truck.

My visible breath, proof that heat could still exist in the frigid cold, reminded me of the days when the three of us used to walk to the park. We'd run through with Hannah's laser guns, even in the winter. Especially in the winter, because of the colors on the snow.

Sam got the car going—engine, heat, radio. "I wish I had

seat warmers," he mumbled.

Hannah's dad had been the first to get seat warmers, and the three of us, after that, always asked him for a ride to the mall.

"Thinking about Hannah again?" he asked.

"What?"

"You used to get like this before, whenever I'd bring up how we should be together." He reached over and took my ungloved hand in his. "Now you get like that after practice, or when something reminds you of her."

"Everything reminds me of her," I muttered, angry at myself.

He didn't reply.

"I want ice cream," I said, when what I really wanted was to drift back in time to before anything ever went bad. Back when it was still the three of us. Before we'd hurt each other.

"It's freezing outside."

"It's warm in the drugstore."

Shrinking inside my coat, as small and covered as I could be, I watched the suburb as it went by. Whitewashed and spindly, the landscape this time of year was more Whitney than Hannah. Thin and pale versus bright and robust. Whitney had always liked being covered up—*cozy,* she'd say—whenever Hannah argued that she was looking frumpy or trying to talk her out of a sweatshirt. Cold on the outside but warm on the inside, where I was starting to think Hannah was maybe the opposite.

Sam parked along the curb in front of the library, and I opened the car door, letting the frosty air seep around and through me. My boots hit the thin layer of snow and ice with a crunch, and the jingle of chimes brought us into a world of time past and magic present. Ironically, this was what it took to clear my head.

Taking a deep breath of the dusty memories, I smiled at Sam. "Hannah can do this ice cream thing much better than I can, but I'll give you a tutorial anyway."

He leaned in to kiss my earlobe. I turned abruptly to him, inclining my head toward the ancient pharmacist watching us. "He sees everything," I whispered.

The one time Whitney had thought about stealing something, he was behind us in a flash. Speedier than you would think any white-haired, not-so-able-bodied adult could be. I'm telling you, the time continuum in here was questionable.

"Okay, so the ice cream cone," I said, sweeping over to the machine.

"Yes, the ice cream cone."

I handed him one. "You go up and down, sort of fast. Not slow, and not jerky, and not around and around. You have to sort of push the cone up into the ice cream. If you go too slow and don't push at all, then you're just building a skinny tower that'll never make it out the door. Around and around is only useful if you're using a cup and a hollow center doesn't matter. Packing it in, making it stable, it takes this special handiwork." I showed him. Not quite of Hannah caliber, but not bad, either. "Now you try."

Immediately, he started twirling. It was gut instinct, everyone did it.

I groaned, held his wrist with my spare hand, and helped. "Like that."

"Please," Hannah's voice muttered from behind me. "You can't stop at three inches."

I stiffened and turned. Jon and Sam greeted each other with silent nods, and Hannah stood in front of me with a straight face. It was hard to read for once, composed and hesitant.

"I mean, unless you want to, I guess," she amended. "If you only want three inches, I shouldn't force you to eat seven, just because I want to show off."

"Exactly," I said.

"Isn't this the place with the lollies?" Jon asked, his eyes darting up to the counter, a very *not*-sly way of coaxing Sam up there to leave Hannah and me alone.

Sam raised his ice cream and slid an arm around me. "I'm good, man. You go get your lolly."

Jon shrugged and rested an arm up on the whirring ice cream machine.

Hannah took a step toward me, fingers fidgety in her hair. "I'm sorry."

"I know you are," I replied. She'd already said so in a

handful of different ways.

"But you're not listening."

"I hear you. I'm just not sure it's enough."

"What would be enough?" Her voice cracked as the frustration eked through—because she wasn't in control, because it wasn't going her way.

"I don't know."

"Marin, come on." Her left side crumbled, hip tilting to let everything else fall. She stood before me, weakened and vulnerable and begging me to rebuild her with words of affirmation and reassurances and... How had I always thought she was my first line of defense? Maybe, this whole time, I was really her first line of self-esteem, the way I'd built her up whenever she wavered. I'd always thought of myself in her shadow, but maybe it had been me holding her out in front, propping her weight on my strength the whole time.

"There has to be something," she insisted.

"I don't know what's going to make me feel better, and I'm not about to sit around and worry about it just because it's bothering you."

"But Marin, we're... We're *us*."

"Whitney and Hannah and Marin were an *us* too. And you didn't care how anyone else felt about it. When you were ready for it to end, it ended. Maybe this time, it's not going to be your choice."

She glared at me for a minute, and I about wanted to

shove my cone in her face—I shouldn't be getting any glares right now, that's for damn sure, not after what she did—but then I realized she was trying not to cry, her eyes unnaturally wide and gleaming.

Shit. I had to get out of there. Hurrying past her, I threw five dollars on the counter. If there was one thing I wasn't going to let myself do, it was forgive her only because I felt guilty for making her feel bad.

The cold slapped some sense into me, and I took an icy breath.

Tossing my uneaten cone in the trash, I turned around as the store spit out Sam, my change outstretched in his palm. Ignoring it and reaching under his jacket instead for the waistband of his jeans, I pulled him to me, my knuckles rubbing against the soft skin of his hip.

Sam nestled his face against my neck. His breath came out in heaves against the soft cotton of my scarf, billowing the fabric, tickling my skin.

"I'm so glad you picked me," he muttered, as I squirmed, the fifteen degrees of chill climbing back through me and clashing with Sam's hot exhales.

"Who else would I have picked?"

He looked at me a moment, then replied, "Hannah."

Had I picked Sam, though? I'd wanted to, but until Hannah was revealed as a lying, manipulating, little shit, I hadn't. Would I have, eventually? I wasn't sure.

I would now, though. I would today and tomorrow, and if

nothing else, he was the impetus for me to figure out how to pull my life from under her thumb.

Why should my life be under someone else's thumb? How had that ever seemed like a good idea?

We crossed the street and slid into his truck, and I remembered that today was supposed to be for us, not my memories and my friends and the hurt that swelled when I thought of them. Knowing Sam could sear my thoughts away, I stopped his hand from shifting the truck into gear and pulled his face to mine.

Chapter 18

...or present.

THE NEXT TIME HANNAH came in to work to see Sam, things were totally different.

First, I was in the aisle with him, on the same side and working off the same dolly, and we weren't in a suspended state of awkward flirting but a heightened state of easy laughter.

It stopped her at the end cap, and she stared at us for a moment. Could she tell I was beyond satiated? Gluttonously stuffed to nearly bursting, with bits of thick cotton leaking out at every seam?

Looking down, I could almost see the soft white wisps where I might pluck them from myself. Hannah had always been maniacal about her stuffed animals—no filling could show, and she would pull and pull and pull at the bits until her friends were a weak, floppy version of themselves.

Good thing Whit and I had walked away from that so long ago.

Shaking her hair out—a tic I knew Hannah used to imbibe confidence—she came toward us.

"Hey, Hannah," Sam said, the smile on his face, an obvious leftover of our conversation, fading the closer she got.

"Hey." Her gaze flittered toward me, like she knew where I stood and that she'd been officially knocked off the runner-up platform. "Why does it always smell like a bakery in here? It doesn't matter what aisle—produce, diapers, chips, candy. All of it, bakery."

"Sometimes the fried chicken takes over—that's nice. And there's always the cardboard." I held up an empty box to her. "Can't you smell the cardboard? Crushed and weeping, wet and miserable? Do you know what happens to these boxes back there? *Torture*."

Sam chuckled, taking the box from me and bopping my folded knee with it. "What's up?" he asked her.

She sighed through a bland, unamused facial expression and turned from me to him. "I was wondering if you were going to Jon's to watch the game."

"We have plans," I told her.

"It's the World Cup finals," she snipped. "Do you know your boyfriend at all?"

I glanced at Sam. He'd been talking about the World Cup for weeks. "You should go."

"I don't want to," he replied, so quick it was clearly something he'd already considered.

I fumbled with the cans I was trying to stock—too many at once—and they started to topple. Catching them, but smashing my pinky in the process, I cursed.

"She can come with," Hannah offered dryly. "And her dirty mouth, too."

"What a lovely offer," I muttered.

He motioned to my hand, cradled in my lap. "It looks like I have a wound to attend to."

She heaved a sigh. "I'll tell Jon to order pizza for both of you."

"Just for Sam should be good."

Sam shook his head at me. "I can always watch soccer, but I get limited time with you."

He had a point. We were a collection of moments between extra practices for the team dances Imani had strong-armed me into, studio time perfecting my solos, homework, and work. Fifteen minutes of our break. Forty-five after work. Twenty at the end of the night in the studio parking lot. Five after school. Three in the school hallways between class.

"Even so, you shouldn't give up your friends or your hobbies."

"Playing soccer is my hobby, not watching it. And you are my most important friend."

"Ugh, you guys. I get it, okay? Marin wins. Like always." Spinning, she stalked down the aisle only to turn back at the end. "We'll order pizza for both of you, just in case."

When there was no longer a trace of her, not even the trail or whisper or aura of her hair, I tossed a box at him and laughed. "'I have a wound to attend to?'"

"She seems kind of mad at you."

"Yeah, I don't have any idea what I ever won that she cares two shits about."

"Me, Marin Greene." He leaned over, planting hands on either side of my knees. "You won me."

"Sam Hanson." I scoffed. "You are not a trophy. Have some self-respect."

With a grin, he leaned in so close that our noses almost touched, and I tried to keep my breathing steady. *We were at work.* But the air pulsed around us, caught up in a heartbeat of its own like we could make magic out of oxygen.

"Kiddles!" Kesh cried from the end of the aisle, causing us both to jump about three feet. "Stop the snarfling."

"We do not snarfle," I objected. In all the ways Sam touched me, always trying to keep up contact, there was in each an unfolding and an unfurling. Then a kiss would send me springing back, curling like a ribbon razed with a blade. Then a finger tracing my spine, unspooling. A kiss, and a touch, back and forth and again and again. There was so much more to it than a stupid snarfle. "Snarfle is not a very pleasant-sounding word," I pointed out.

Kesh ignored me. "Are we doing this?"

Sam checked his watch and stood to pile our empty boxes on top of the one we didn't get to.

I, however, was still stuck on the word snarfle. Thinking of the last few weeks, an inkblot spread across my senses in a dark bloom, bruising along my edges where I'd been tenderized.

Snarfle? No. Absolutely not. As much as I liked made-up words, this was not an accurate observation.

And then it occurred to me. As Sam led the dolly into the back room, Kesh at his side and me trailing after them as they talked about college letters that were starting to flow in and which of Kesh's fifty-five options he was leaning toward, it occurred to me that I was arguing with myself that Sam and I meant more than a stupid, simple snarfle.

The irony.

"Hey, Kesh?" I asked as we walked onto the dock out back. They turned. "Sam and I have a soccer game to get to."

Sam shook his head. "You're taking us to the park. We've been planning this all week, this famous spot in the park."

"We're watching the World Cup with your friends."

"Not until you take us to the park. Then maybe we can catch the second half."

Fine, okay, that sounded like a decent compromise. At least, until we weren't the only ones with the same idea. Whit and Vic were parked in my normal spot.

So she missed us, too, even though she'd been ignoring my calls and avoiding me at school. Sam pulled up next to me in his truck as I stepped out to face my best friend. Her lip ring was missing, but stranger yet, her hair was different. Normally parched and desperate for color, it was now closer to her natural tone.

"Hi," I said, slow and steady and cautious.

"Hi." She crossed her arms.

"I'm sorry."

"I know."

"Then why haven't you returned my calls?"

"Because somehow you actually continue to believe that I've been lying to you our entire lives, which is super insulting and doesn't deserve a response."

"You can't see how it might be a logical conclusion to draw?"

"No!" Her nails dug into her arms where she clutched them, and she took a deep breath to calm herself. "No. The logical conclusion is, when you made it clear you wouldn't give Vic a chance, I couldn't tell you the truth."

"You can always tell me the truth."

"I could. Until it was obvious I couldn't."

I shrank against my car as Vic stepped around his to wrap a slithering boa arm across her shoulders. I frowned and, closing my eyes for a minute, tried to remember I wasn't doing this anymore. I was doing hope and faith.

Sam was at my side now, across from Vic, and they nodded at each other.

"Can we talk?" I asked. "Just you and me?"

Moments ticked by as she studied me, gauging, no doubt, whether I was yet worthy of a talk. No, I hadn't earned it, but she nodded anyway and began walking toward the tree line, to our bench.

Vic got back in his car, and I turned to Sam. "You should go to Jon's."

He strummed his fingers along the hood of my car. "Call me when you're done, okay?"

I nodded.

Whit and I were silent the whole walk to the bench—the kind of silent that implied there was space between us. Once we were sitting, both rigid and facing straight ahead, I waited for her to start scolding me for what a brat I'd been. I'd admit it, even if I wouldn't take anything I said back. But she didn't. She just picked at her nails and ran her feet along the dead grass beneath us. Zipping up my coat all the way, I stuffed my hands in my pockets.

A pair of runners beat their way down the path from the right. Two girlfriends that could've been us in ten years—if we'd ever cared about running, which we didn't. They came, they passed, they disappeared.

I didn't have it in me to whistle, and Whit didn't bother with a catcall.

"We sucked that one," she muttered.

"A total fail," I agreed, and we shared a soft smile. "I'm sorry I've been an asshole. But moving in with a stranger, using a guy for an exit plan, you can see how it could make a girl nervous, right?"

She pulled her feet up on the bench and wrapped her arms around her legs. "I get it."

"Do you, though? He's everything you never liked, and

everything you never wanted. Not to mention, he's a little scary-looking."

"Nothing else has ever worked for me. So maybe this will, you know?" She twisted her hair over her shoulder. "And he's only scary-looking in the dark. It's his nose. It's crooked because he was a professional boxer before he went to nursing school."

"You don't want what your parents have," I reminded her.

"Yeah, well, I want something. You're leaving and my mom's leaving, and Miri might be leaving—"

"Wait. What?"

"Yeah, Mom started talking about moving back to Delaware and Dad froze her out of all their bank accounts." She dropped her head back on the bench, her hair falling like a waterfall in the dim light. "She never would've gone, but now that he did that, I think she's actually going to."

"But you don't have to move out, then. If there's no fighting, an exit plan isn't necessary."

"Vic's not just an exit plan, Marin. I can talk to him."

"Are you saying you can no longer talk to me?"

She rocked her head from side to side, as if she wouldn't commit to admitting it, but wouldn't exactly deny it, either. "Because he's truly a decent guy who reads me poetry and has smart things to say and thinks the way I want to think. I'm sure about this, Marin, as best as I can be. I mean, I'm not going to marry him or anything, but I know what I'm getting into. I know people will hate us and my parents might disown me, and Miri will probably try to steal his TV some night when we have her and Steve over and they fall asleep in the living room and we're having sex in the bedroom, but that's okay. I already warned him."

"Hold up." I cleared my throat. "You have already warned him of this exact scenario?"

"You know what he said, Marin? He said, 'For you, I'll buy another TV.' He's not using me. He appreciates me. And he tells me when I'm being stupid. When you're gone, who else is going to do that?"

"*Me.* I'm still going to do that. I'm always going to do that. Don't replace me."

"I'm not replacing you. I just met a boy. I'd take you back in a second if you gave him a chance."

"You met a man." I looked at her sharply. "And you acted like a lovesick idiot, which isn't you."

"I was nervous. And I wanted you to see that I liked him."

"All I saw was that you changed for him. I mean, where's the lip ring and what's with the natural hair color?"

"Oh." She touched her hair. "That's because I filled out an app for a suicide hotline gig."

I smiled a little, at how no one else would put those words together.

"I figured it would look good for college, if I want to go into psychology. Vic suggested it. See? He's a good influence."

Just like any good daddy figure should be. But this time, I successfully bit back my commentary. "I can't believe all this is happening to you, your mom and a job, and I never heard a thing about it."

She shrugged. "Vic got me through it."

Rummaging through my purse, I fished out the sharpest point I could find and twisted around to scratch two more tally marks into the bench.

"What are those for?"

"For kissing that guy at Kesh's party, and for being such a bad friend lately." I paused and looked over at her. "I'm sorry, Whit. I'm sorry I've been doing it all wrong."

"How about we just start over?" she offered.

"Please."

"That means you have to give him a chance, though."

With a sigh, I nodded, coming to terms with it. "I know."

"I could text him to join us right now."

I didn't answer. I swallowed hard and tried to answer, but it didn't work.

"Not ready?" she asked, her voice a little colder again.

"I promised Sam I'd meet him at Jon's for the soccer game."

She stood. "Then I'll walk you back."

"Soon, okay?"

"Sure."

I couldn't do it tonight, I couldn't do it alone, and maybe I couldn't do it at all. I had to, though. I just needed time.

And Sam. Him at my side would help, too.

We were silent the rest of the way to the parking lot, and when we reached the pavement, she said, "Actions speak louder than promises," then slammed the door shut and sealed the two of them together inside.

Chapter 19
Either learning to fight...

IT WAS HARD NOT talking to Hannah while still having to speak to her about any number of things related to the dance team, seeing as we were co-captains, but competition Saturdays were the worst.

It felt most awful not being us when performing. The one time we'd almost danced apart, the day she made it only a few steps into her solo before running off the stage in a blur, I'd taken one look at her suddenly limp hair—as if the life had gone out of her and there it showed—before scrambling down the steps to follow her out to the parking lot, even though this meant missing my own first solo. Hiding behind a blue van, she cried on my shoulder, and we swore we'd never do it again. We'd never dance apart again.

Maybe it should make me bitter, that I could've had a life of solos and glory, but it only made me nostalgic. Dance was what we did together. It was what made us Hannah and Marin in the first place, and possibly what had split Whitney, the other third of the atomic compound, off into obsolescence.

At least today was a local competition, so I wouldn't be stuck in a hotel with her through tomorrow. No team pizza party or hot tub rendezvous to rest our sore muscles.

Since I'd slept at my dad's, I'd driven myself, and the ride was as lazy and silent as the morning. He wasn't up yet but would come later, closer to my performance time.

I parked in a slice of sun peeking over the building and wandered in, knowing well how to find my way. This downtown high school had housed many weekend dance competitions over the years.

My mom was probably already in the crowd, her pen and the paper schedule at the ready. She liked to be there when the doors opened so she didn't miss any performances. She'd make notes for each routine and whenever she spotted us emerging from the halls for food, she'd tell us who was going to beat us. Parents couldn't be in the dressing rooms the way they could at studio comps, so maybe it gave her something to do.

Hannah had already found the classroom that had been designated for us and messaged the team. Something we used to do together because we'd have spent the night at her house and ridden together.

"Marin!" she cried, spotting me as I walked in. She held a coffee out between us, my name slashed in black along the side.

Ignoring it, I dropped my bag on the other end of the

circle from her.

The rest of the team was doing each other's hair and makeup like we'd normally do on the bus if the school was farther away. Since Hannah always did mine, I'd made sure to come ready. Checking over my severe pony—light brown strands individually slicked back with a fine-toothed comb and water—I took another round of hairspray to it, then changed into my uni. Covering that with my team jacket and yoga pants slipped under my skirt, I pulled on fat, fuzzy socks and popped one earbud in my ear, setting our first song on an endless cycle so my subconscious could continue running through it while the rest of me took care of other things.

We had a while before we were up, and girls were running out to grab breakfast now that the concession stand was open, so when my phone buzzed, Sam letting me know he was in the lobby, I told our coach I was making a smoothie run.

I'd given him performance times but told him to show up no earlier than a half hour before because we weren't really allowed out of the back halls. If we weren't watching solos or another team from the area, we were supposed to stay in the dressing room.

When Hannah followed me out, it made sense. She'd probably told Jon to be there all day, and Jon roped Sam into keeping him company. Thanks to me not talking to Hannah, she had pretty much cemented Jon as her new, trusty sidekick. Whatever she'd talked me into doing for and with her on a normal day, now she weaseled Jon into doing.

Her elbow brushed mine as we slid through the dancers coming in. Looking lost in the sea of tight ponies and lipstick, Sam and Jon were propped up against opposite walls at the end of the hall.

Sam laughed a little when he saw me. I pouted and put my hands on my hips. He slid his arms around my waist and pulled me to him, dipping down to whisper-kiss my earlobe. "You hardly look like yourself."

"And that cues laughter?"

"Good laughter. Holy-shit laughter. Not-sure-I-could-pick-you-out-of-a-crowd laughter."

"It looks better on stage."

"It doesn't look bad, it just looks..." He motioned to the rest of the slick-ponied, heavily made-up, uniformed girls of slightly varying heights and widths around us.

"Yes, it's a thing," I agreed, glancing over at Hannah, whose giggling could be heard over the strum of feet passing by and the hushed early-morning whispers. Jon was talking into her ear through a wide smile, and her head dropped back to laugh, hair sagging along her back. She should have it up already.

"Jon couldn't handle being here without a friend?" I asked.

"Hannah told him when the doors opened, and I figured,

why not me, too?"

"Because I didn't want to torment you like that."

"It's not torment to support my girlfriend."

"You can support me just as well in a few hours."

"Marin, I don't mind doing things for you. In fact, I kind of like it."

"But I can't stay with you."

"I know. You should be with your team. I totally get it."

"And you're standing over here, instead of over there by him, because of me?"

He nodded. "I didn't want you to be uncomfortable."

I kissed him as lightly as I could, so as not to transfer or ruin my lipstick, then led him by hand through the current to Hannah's side. I wasn't going to have things be weird between Sam and Jon because of me. And it was time to get to work.

"Come on," I said to her. "You need to get your hair up."

After awards and a few pictures, the team split up to find our friends and families. My dad found me first, wrapped me up, and kissed me on the forehead. "You were brilliant."

"Thanks, Dad."

"Should've taken the whole thing."

My mom appeared behind him. "I don't know," she said. "That first-place team had unbelievable energy."

We both ignored her. "You hungry?" he asked me. It was close to ten, but yes, I was starving.

"I am," my mom replied. "Maybe I want to celebrate, too."

I snorted. Going to eat with my divorced parents who could hardly speak civilly to each other? Was she seriously suggesting this?

"You didn't even think she should have won," my dad pointed out. "You're not sounding very celebratory."

"When have I ever sounded celebratory?" she replied, which caused him to laugh. An actual laugh from my suit-and-tie-wearing dad was something of a unicorn sighting. It made my mom's face twist. "What's that supposed to mean?"

I tried to center. If I was tranquil enough, it would pass. My dad would not choose to battle. I would not choose to battle. She would have no one to do business with and would deflate soon enough.

My dad put his palms up as white flags, while bringing his amusement to an effective close. His face flashed like he was trying to hide another smile. "For once, you're accurately self-assessing."

"Dad," I warned. But at least his demeanor was calm, cool, and collected. Looking at him on approach, you wouldn't think tension was snaking its way through the three of us.

And Sam, of all people, was actually approaching. He slipped his hand into mine, squeezing once. "You deserved first."

My mom rolled her eyes, and I took a deep breath, trying to work seamlessly into an introduction that might very well lead to the apocalypse. I could see the headlines now: Polite Boyfriend Sets Off Irritated Mother Zombie in Kansas City.

"Mom, this is Sam. Sam, my mom."

She sized him up and looked at me. "You're not going to introduce him to your father?"

"We've already met," my dad said, and I couldn't help but note the tinge of neener-neener in his voice.

Setting my hand to my belly, I realized that it ached, and not because I was hungry. Stupid parents. I survived an entire day with Hannah, and this is what unravels me? Three minutes with my parents side by side?

"I may not demand to know where she goes every minute of every day," my dad said, "but I make sure I know the people she's spending her time with."

Enter the age-old argument of how to parent me, a girl who barely even needed parenting, thank you very much. I battened down the hatches as my mom wound up—standing taller, leaning forward, breathing in until the air filled the fists at her sides to great proportions.

"Hi, family!" Hannah bounced through the impending bubble of doom like it couldn't affect her.

I squeezed tighter to Sam's hand, anchoring him from the shock and discomfort. Or anchoring me, it was hard to tell.

"How *is* everybody? We did great, right? Didn't you think, Mrs. Greene?" Hannah shook out her hair, which had been immediately ripped free of the pony on the way off stage.

"Well..." But it was a daring feat to disagree with the challenge of Hannah's raised eyebrow.

"How is everyone?" Hannah continued, leaving just enough time to make them think they could answer, but not enough that they actually could. "What's new? I hear Marin got into Wash U. So amazing, you guys should be so proud. I am, *of course*. Even though it means she's leaving me."

"She hasn't gotten into Wash U," my mom piped up, her spine straightening rigid. If I had wings, she would clip them. And clip them and clip them and clip them. Daily, probably, just to make sure I wouldn't be able to make it across the street, let alone the four hours to Wash U.

"I haven't heard yet," I admitted, trying to ignore this punch in the stomach. Aside from the fact that I should have, my dad had doubled down on not paying for room and board. Said it was important to have some skin in the game. Which meant, if Wash U didn't pan out, I probably would end up at KU with Hannah, since they offered me enough money to cover living in the dorms. K-State would be harder to figure out, and my dad was also adamant that college shouldn't put you into debt. He said there was no reason I couldn't just live with him. I didn't bother telling him that the reason I couldn't do that was that he lived three streets away from my mother.

"Don't look so worried. I'm sure you'll get in." Hannah leaned her head toward me with certainty as she said it, and that certainty filled me before I could stop it.

Right. They'd probably gotten me mixed up with the second early-action deadline, which meant I would hear by mid-February. Or I'd call on Monday. They were probably just behind. Everyone was these days.

My mom eyeballed Hannah. "You really shouldn't get her hopes up," she said.

"Okay, so Jon's waiting for us," Hannah said to my parents. As if Sam and I already knew about it. I looked at him, but he was in a bit of a daze. Right. Of course. I hadn't prepared him.

Hannah rolled her eyes and grabbed hold of my arm. "We're gonna run. I'll have Marin home by curfew, promise!" And she jerked me away as my parents started arguing about what time that should be.

Not about who I was eating with. No one had really cared if I celebrated with them or not, they just wanted to win.

Too caught in this realization, I didn't fight Hannah as

she led me out to the curb where Jon's SUV was idling.

Letting go, she faced me. "Please, Marin? Have dinner with us? Maybe we could even do the hot tub later, like we would if we were out of town. My mom's really been missing you, too. She made your favorite cookies last night, just in case."

"She only makes Kris Kringles before Christmas," I pointed out.

"Well, she now also makes them for you."

"I'm starving!" Jon shouted, out the window.

She nodded so hard her hair may as well have been on a trampoline. That had been how we'd gotten our aerials—day after day after night on the trampoline in her backyard.

If only I could look at her or hear her name or live my life without the memories.

"I made reservations at that Greek restaurant you like," she whispered. "For four."

Hannah hated Mediterranean food. Straight Italian was as close as she'd get.

"What are you going to eat?" I wondered, curiosity making me pause.

"You can order for me."

"Hummus and stuffed grape leaves?"

She stifled the gag. The thought of grape leaves did that to her. And hummus. "I'll eat every bite, if only you'll forgive me—no, you don't even have to forgive me, you just have to give me a night, for starters, please?"

I crossed my arms, hugging myself against the cold.

"Okay, even if you don't forgive me, I'll just eat it for all the things I've made you do over the years." She looked hard at me for a moment, then dropped her gaze to her feet, swiping one toe out and over, an old ballet move we'd lost inside the pop of poms.

Well, it was a start. Admissions, maybe that's all I wanted. Her admitting that perhaps there was another reality outside the one she'd created for us.

But so many of the steps I'd made toward her in the past had felt like cutting a finger off. Or at least a lock of hair—maybe it didn't really hurt, but it was still something I'd lost. Not something I'd necessarily miss, but after you do it enough times and you have no hair left, then you feel it. The cold wind on a bare head. The lack of protection and the lack of shelter.

I was trying to grow my hair back in.

"I'm more in the mood for tacos," I admitted. And it would still be a compromise for Hannah, a lock of hair off her head. She thought tacos were boring, but of course this was her assessment of the American version—hard shell, ground beef with powder seasoning, cheddar cheese, and lettuce—while I preferred the real deal with a corn tortilla, shredded meat, chopped onions, and cilantro.

"Of course," Hannah beamed. And it lit a small spark in her eye. "Yes. Tacos."

"But we're driving separately." And I stalked off toward my car.

I was quiet on the way, and as soon as I parked, Hannah wrenched open the door, dragged me out, and squeezed me tight.

"Thank you for this," she said, in the most sincere, honest tone I'd ever heard her use. It was the one that came in the dark as she relayed her nightmares—deep, dark things with fangs and claws, prevalent and swooping—surprisingly so, considering she was a girl with such a positive attitude. It was also the one she'd used to cut Whitney free of us when Whit had finally confronted us and I could only speak in tears and sorrow and regret. She'd used it after the solo debacle, too, when faced with her most embarrassing fears and failings. "I love you," she added.

Then she bounded away and opened the door of the taqueria for us to file in.

It was the watchful eye she had on me during dinner that was the final blow. As if I was in the habit of tossing eggshells in a tantrum and taunting people to walk on them if they dared to reach me, which was the opposite of what I'd ever wanted to be. The horror of making people feel that way was a feeling I knew all too well.

It clawed at me, and I broke. So, when she asked, warily, if I'd go to the bathroom with her... I mean, I did have to pee, but *of course. Don't look at me that way. I can't have anyone looking at me that way.*

"Know what I was thinking about the other day?" she asked, as the door swung shut behind us. "Remember when your parents took us to that cabin for the weekend?"

I slipped into a stall. We'd been twelve. I remembered.

"That boy two houses down? Your parents invited him over for dinner after they found out we thought he was cute?"

My parents had caught all three of us—Hannah, Whitney, and me—watching him fish. We were sitting there, staring, and they'd started teasing us.

It had been one of the few times they'd done something together.

Then they'd cooked dinner together, to music, and we could hear their laughter through the windows as we watched the boy.

"He stayed for marshmallows and stargazing..." she called over the partition.

I'd forgotten his name, but I remembered that day. I'd thought that maybe we'd be happier if my parents bought a cabin.

"And we fought until dawn over who we thought he liked." The toilet flushed. "You remember?"

"I remember." He'd liked Whitney, I was pretty sure. Hannah thought he liked her, of course, and Whitney agreed. But since Hannah always stood in front, it was the obvious assumption to make.

"Your mom made us the best pancakes with strawberries

and M&M's, and we thought for sure she'd lost her mind."

On happiness. We'd thought she'd lost her mind on happiness. She'd never doled out the M&M's like everyone else's parents. *Sugar, the root of all evil.*

My dad refused to give me that cabin, so my mom started teaching yoga, instead of just doing it. She said it was to be our vacation money, only then we never went on vacation.

I'd thought maybe she was teaching yoga for me, for that cabin, but then again, maybe it was one of those things we'd both wanted.

Hannah kept going, but I stopped listening. She was reliving our glory days so I'd be more inclined to forgive and forget—this was her closing argument, I knew—but next to the memories of my parents, it had me wondering about Whitney. Hannah was conveniently leaving her name out of it, but I was focused on the girl I used to know.

For the first time, I wondered if I'd picked the wrong best friend. "Hannah." I cleared my throat as we met up at the sinks. "I am going to Wash U, if I get in."

Her face fell but bounced right back. "I know, Marin. Of course." Shaking her hands out and reaching for the towels, she added, "It's a great school and I wouldn't want to hold you back. I'm sorry if I have."

The first number of the combination lock on the Hannah locker inside my soul slid into place. She caught me looking at her, the softest face I'd surely had since it all went down that Sunday morning, and she smiled. "I have Jon to hold back now." Then she started laughing. "Just kidding. He was planning on going to KU, though. So that makes it okay, right?"

I grinned. "For four years, anyway, that makes it okay."

"Good." She nodded with a small smile.

"I just thought you should know, about Wash U," I said as we swung out the door. Because what I needed her to hear was something I couldn't say without feeling like I was slicing through her Achilles tendon: *I will no longer, no matter if we make up, be making decisions based on yours.*

In this, I almost felt like a different person for a second, a version of me who wouldn't have put up with all the things I'd put up with. I bathed in that empowerment for a moment because I knew it was going to slip away.

And it did. But it was a moment to hold onto at least, for the next time I might need it.

Chapter 20

...or learning to fold.

IT WAS QUIET AT the competitions on Friday nights with only solos and duets on the schedule, and I had the classroom-turned-dressing room almost to myself.

I worked my hair into a fat, teased Dutch braid, then added fake eyelashes to my smoky eye make-up. Lipliner, to keep the lipstick in place, and a deep rouge on my cheeks. All so my features wouldn't get washed out under the bright lights. You didn't want to give the judges any reason to look away from you. Last were my sparkly earrings—studs of significant size, because to notice something on stage it had to be ten times what it was off stage.

"You look amazing," said a voice from behind me.

I swung around on my stool to find Hannah.

Looking around at the nearly empty room that would have dance moms elbowing for space tomorrow, she said, "I wanted to call a truce."

"You came here to call a truce?"

She ran her hand along the back of the chair in front of

me. "I shouldn't have stormed off the other night, and I shouldn't have let you get to me. I've been trying to be the better person. You know, include the new girlfriend so the friend doesn't disappear forever."

"So, for your sake, you included me."

"For Sam's sake," she corrected.

"And for Sam's sake, you're calling a truce."

"Maybe. Does it matter?"

I didn't care if we called a truce or not, so it shouldn't matter what her reasoning was, but her folding for the sake of my boyfriend felt fake, like most everything she'd done the last few years.

"What did you mean the other night, that I always win?" I asked.

She laughed. "You're kidding, right?"

Her hair was lit up like a halo, illuminating how she had always been the chosen one, the golden child. "No, I'm not kidding."

"You got the solos, the glory, the friend, and now the guy. You fight for everything, and you always win, no matter how hard I try."

"You're joking."

"How is any of that a joke?"

"You're the star!" I cried. "The doted-on only child. Your parents love you and love you and love you. Everyone loves you. You have this...this...I don't know, this light, this charm that pulls everyone in. How can you be jealous of me?" It was so obvious I couldn't imagine how she wouldn't know the effect she had on people.

"Well, first, thank you very much for the kind words." She flashed a grin, and I snorted a little. "Second, you're the one with all the talent. And the follow-through. I just go with what's easy." She diverted her gaze to my second solo costume, hanging off a hook on the wall. "Which is fine, usually. Only this time I worked for something and didn't get it."

"Sam?"

Clearing her throat, she played it off in a way that even I could find halfway adorable. "Hey," she brightened, "want me to help you stretch?"

"Really?"

She smirked. "You know me, always in the mood to inflict a little pain."

I slid off my stool onto the floor, motioning her over. Imani wasn't here yet, Sam was nearly useless in this category, Whit had her interview for the shelter so wasn't able to make it, and my mom was already in the auditorium judging other soloists. No way she'd leave her post at this point.

Hannah slid her hands onto the top of my foot. "Imani might hire me for a pom workshop this spring," she said.

"Yeah? You guys keep in touch?"

"Why do you think I'm here? Anyway, maybe you and I will be working together again."

"That would be interesting."

"I can put it all behind us if you can." She pushed a little harder.

I winced. "How big of you."

"More?"

Biting my lip, I nodded.

"I do miss this."

"Inflicting pain?"

She winked. "No, helping others."

I laughed and with a grin, she eased back, switching to my other foot. "So, you're going to go to K-State with Sam?"

"No, Chapman. I was hoping to do their dance program."

"Wow. That's amazing, Marin."

How amazing it would have been chewed up my stomach. "Callbacks are this month, and I haven't heard." I should call on Monday. Not that I thought I had a shot at the dance school any longer, but that meant no talent scholarship, which I wasn't sure I wanted to face quite yet. I was pretty sure that without it, I'd never be able to make it work. "I want to be in L.A. if I can. Train at the studios there."

"If anyone can make it in L.A., it's you."

I raised an eyebrow at her. "Maybe you should wait to assess until after you watch me perform tonight."

"I've seen you perform," she said.

"Eight years ago, maybe."

"Not true. I make it to almost every Studio One competition I can."

"You do not."

"Yes, I do! Imani always sends me the schedule. I don't stick around to congratulate anyone because no one even knows me anymore."

"Why bother?"

She shrugged as we started on the second round of my first foot. "Trying to figure out if that solo of mine could have gone any differently, maybe. Or what might have happened if you'd have come after me."

"I couldn't come after you; I was up next."

"I would have come after you."

I nearly snorted at that, and she stretched my foot another painful notch to make me wince.

"Oh, shut up. Fine. Maybe I wouldn't have."

"I'll let you think so if you go a little easier on me."

But she didn't, like I knew she wouldn't, because she knew I didn't really want her to.

I sighed. It was empowering dancing alone, but there was something about this too, something I'd missed. Hannah pulled on my heel, turned my foot, and pushed up while I pushed down. So easy, so familiar.

"So, all I had to do to get you to be nice again was steal your boyfriend?"

She gave me a look. "It's not like you and Whitney were ever peaches and cream, either."

I laughed out loud, and she rewarded me with a short, pursed smile, the kind she rewarded people with when she was pleased. How did I remember that? How could all these things be the same as all those years ago? How could there have been so much distance between us when really there wasn't?

I guess we'd been friends when our personalities were being formed. We'd known each other's secrets when we chose our paths, even if we'd chosen different ones. If nothing else, she knew why I was me as much as I knew why she was her, and clearly there was something to be said about that.

She stretched me out in silence for a few more minutes, and when my second foot was as close to the ground as it could go, I said, "You haven't lost your touch."

"Thanks," she grinned. "Maybe there's hope for me after all."

Everyone swarmed me as I came off-stage after the solo awards, two trophies in hand—first place for hope and fifth for anguish.

Judges were generally the positive type.

"Surprised you did so well," my mom said. "There were some truly talented soloists tonight."

I took in a deep breath, letting this comment travel down and settle into my fingertips. I wouldn't be the start of a scene here, where so many people knew me, or knew of me—kids I taught and their parents, along with competitors who'd kept an eye on me over the years, who I also kept an eye on, knowing I had to be better than them to win.

"What are you talking about?" my dad asked. "She was an angel up there."

"I think you should've gotten first place for Anguish, too," Sam said. Anguish and Hope were not the official names of my solos, but it's what he'd taken to calling them.

Hannah stepped up behind him and peeked her head around like she was peering into a private room. "I agree, even though I know it doesn't work like that."

"Thanks." I smiled. Then to my parents, who were looking a little confused, I explained. "Hannah helped me stretch earlier."

She entered the circle then, as if my thanks were permission, and sent a big beaming smile at me, flashed it next at my parents, and then toward Sam. "And," Hannah added, "with the reassessment in, you are absolutely a solid for the Chapman dance program."

"She hasn't gotten in yet," my mom said.

Sam reached over to squeeze my hand. "She will."

"You shouldn't be telling people that, Marin, if you don't know."

"She didn't tell me that, Mrs. Greene," Hannah said. "It's just obvious."

My dad stepped forward and cleared his throat. "I'm Mr. Greene," he stuck his hand out toward Sam. "And you are?"

"Oh! Sorry. Dad, this is Sam. Sam, my dad." He'd met my mom that night at the studio, back when he'd asked me to Homecoming.

"Nice to meet you." Sam offered a hand, and they shook.

"Do you have college plans?"

"I got a free ride to K-State for soccer, but if Marin ends up at KU, I might consider going there instead."

My attention jumped to him—as did Hannah's—and I tried to do that probing insect thing he did to fig-ure out if he had caught on to the let's-see-how-riled-we-can-get-Mrs. Greene game or if he was actually being serious. Because this was the first he'd mentioned it to me, leaving the free ride behind for my sake, and hell if I was going to let him do that. Not to mention, I threw up a little in my mouth at the thought of going to KU, even though they'd pay the difference I needed to be able to live in the dorms without any loans, which my dad was also against. It was like he was unwittingly blocking every road out.

Hannah broke the silence. "They don't even have men's soccer at KU, Sam."

He shrugged. "They have club."

My mom made a strangled noise. "One should never make decisions based on a high-school sweetheart. Throwing away a scholarship for some girl is idiocy."

Some girl. My mom had just referred to me as *some girl.* Well, that about summed it up.

"Weren't you two high-school sweethearts?" Hannah asked, so innocently I could almost swear she didn't know the can of worms she'd unleashed.

I didn't know what was happening tonight, but this Hannah, the one who'd stretched me out and was now goading my mom with a fiery prod while still pulling off complete innocence? I kind of missed her.

Maybe it was not having Whitney.

My mom leaned in toward Sam. "Trust me, kid, don't marry your high-school sweetheart."

"Thank you, Elizabeth," my dad said. "That's lovely."

"I'm just saying, he might think Marin's great, but sooner or later..."

I imagined a swirling wind whisking me away from this. And for a second, I almost felt like a different person, like a version of me who would have put up with it, a version who respected others and valued self-control. I bathed in the peace of that for a moment because I knew it was going to slip away.

And it did. "Screw you, Mom."

"All I'm saying is that marriage can mess with a person, and I don't think you're really the type to be able to handle it."

"Don't be stupid." I snapped. "Does it look like I'm about to run off and get married?"

"Just ignore her," my dad said.

My mom scoffed. "And surely, ignoring me helps our relationship—is that what you think?"

"It helps me," my dad muttered. "And sometimes that's all I have control over."

"Thanks for making this about you guys," I muttered, grabbing for Sam's hand and the escape while I saw it.

I shared a look with Hannah as Sam and I snuck away, an old look that flooded me with something super confusing as we went our separate ways.

"I'm sorry about that marriage talk," I said, once Sam and I were alone at the park.

He'd been game the moment I mentioned how much I missed it—which was probably more about missing Whit—but like the big brother he was, he insisted we dress for the weather. He'd packed scarves and hats and mittens. Even a blanket.

"It does make a little more sense now, why I practically

had to twist your arm to get you to be monogamously not in a relationship with me."

Pushing out a melodramatic sigh, I said, "I think you could just say it."

"Say what?" he asked.

"That we're together."

He grinned wide and wrapped us up tighter together under the blanket. "Say it again, Marin Greene. Wait. What's your middle name?"

"Eliza. What's yours?"

"Ritter."

I curled against his side as best I could. "Samuel Ritter Hanson, we *are* together. As a wise man once told me, a relationship simply is what it is, no matter what you might think or want it to be."

"Are you saying, Marin Eliza Greene, that you're a wise man's girlfriend?" He dipped his lips to my neck. "That we might *mean* something to each other?" With his nose, he brushed my hair out of the way.

"All right, all right," I muttered weakly. "You're having way too much fun with this."

"So, if I asked you to a dance?" he whispered in my ear, a husky tone I didn't think I could ever turn down.

"I'd go," I admitted, wrapping my arms around his neck.

"Because I'd love to take you to prom."

"Shit."

He laughed into my hair.

"It's a bit early for talk of prom, isn't it?"

"Does that mean you won't go?"

"I don't know. You'd have to ask me all proper-like, for starters."

He pulled away to look at me. "I'm not sure what that means, coming from you."

"It'll be fun watching you try and figure it out," I said, gathering him back up.

Footsteps sounded from beyond the trees, and I perked up. "Shoot. Sam, we didn't go over this one, very important thing."

"You're not backing out already, are you?"

"No. Listen. Runners, right?"

"Sure."

"I announce the stats and you catcall."

"I'm sorry?"

"Just, think up a good catcall."

"That sounds like harassment."

"It's okay, no one's pressed charges yet." I let go of him to brace myself on the bench. Then they rounded the bend.

Bulky arms, bald head. Yoga pants, wheat-blonde hair.

Yoga pants?

I choked and started coughing on the words that had been in my throat at the ready. Sam asked if I was okay, but all I could do was gape.

She came to a running stop in front of me. *Whitney was jogging in place in front of me.*

"Hey." She tried out a soft smirk. Because she had to know how comical this was.

"What are you doing?" I asked.

"Keeping my muscles warm."

Vic was running the perimeter of the clearing on this side of the running trail, circling around us like a carrion bird.

"That's not what I mean."

"We didn't have a chance to run yet today."

"It's Friday night," I pointed out.

"Every day is for running." She grinned. "Just like you think every day is for dancing. I am a little disappointed, though. No stats? No catcall? Weak."

"Yeah, maybe next time."

"How'd the competition go?" she asked.

"First and fifth."

"Wish I could've seen it. But I got the job!"

"Yay! Congrats! We should be celebrating!" And if I'd given Vic a chance yet, maybe we would be. With the start of the dance season, though, I hadn't had time.

"I am celebrating," she said.

I gave her a look. "With a run?"

She stuck her tongue out at me. "You guys wanna come over in a bit? We just need to get home and shower. We could celebrate proper then, both of us."

Vic came around the side of the bench to run in place next to her, his expression nothing if not eager.

"Okay," I said. "We'll be over in an hour."

Bending down so her hair fell like a curtain against my face, she wrapped me in a hug and whispered, "Thank you."

Sam and I sat on a bench that was supposed to be sacred to Whit and me, watching her run off with a man. There were so many things wrong in that moment, I felt like it had been sewn together by an amateur, with seams that clearly didn't fit.

"What am I supposed to do about him?" I wondered, thinking that Hannah would know. Hannah would know what to do about him.

"What can you do?" Sam asked.

"I don't know, but I have to do something, don't I?"

"Why? Why can't you just sometimes *not* do something? You know, sometimes things actually work out."

"You mean us, don't you?"

But he only smiled at the fat spruce across the way.

"Does that mean you like him?"

"I don't know him. But at least she's eighteen now."

Okay, fair point.

"I'm just saying, maybe she'll come to the conclusion you want her to on her own, if you just give her some time."

I turned my head to him. "Is that also in reference to us?"

"Geez, Marin." He scoffed lightly, put an arm around me, and pressed his lips to my hair. "It's not always about us, okay?"

"Sam, you can't give up your scholarship to K-State."

"It was just a thought."

"A crazy thought. That you threw out in front of my parents?"

"I thought they might like it."

I laughed. "How little you know."

"Clearly. God forbid a boy be romantic about their daughter."

"Right?" I snickered. "No one would want you to throw your life away on some girl."

"I think a life would be perfectly wasted on you."

"Oh, shut up," I muttered, burying my face in his scarf. "Promise me you'll go do your soccer thing." Sneaking my hand out from my mitten, I pulled his scarf away from his neck to kiss him there. "Who knows if we'll even still be together then, anyway."

"I know." Lifting my chin, he looked at me with the kind of intensity that shook fault lines across my senses.

"How?" I asked. "How do you know?" How could he be so sure? Nothing was a given in this life.

Reaching his arm past me, he ran his fingers along the initials I'd carved in the bench long ago, maybe only a month or so into my employment at Fiesta.

Pressing one pad hard into the SH, he whispered, "Because you like me, and you always have."

Chapter 21

Either lost...

January had clicked over to February, and I still hadn't heard anything from Wash U. Still hadn't called them, either. But once mid-February hit, I could no longer avoid the fact that their early-decision deadline had passed. Everyone else had gotten either rejection notifications or acceptance letters.

All our friends had heard from and committed to all of their schools. Sam would officially be playing soccer for K-State, and Jon would be at KU with Hannah.

"Good morning, Washington University Admissions."

This was the third time I'd dialed their number, and the second I'd let it ring. "Um, hi. I was wondering about an application for this coming fall?"

"The deadline has passed, my dear."

"Oh, I'm sorry. I don't mean I want to apply. I mean I haven't heard back."

"All acceptance letters have been sent."

I swallowed hard and forced out my next sentence. "But

I haven't gotten a rejection, either."

"What's the name?"

"Marin Greene. M-A-R-I-N, and Greene with an E at the end."

"Hold on, please, while I check."

"Thank you."

The music on the line was a stampede of elephants in sync with my erratic heartbeat. Panic crawled up my throat, the kind that physically aches, and I closed my eyes, praying they only sent paper letters and it had gotten lost in the mail. I was in, of course. *Welcome to Wash U*, she'd say.

"I'm sorry, Marin, but we don't show that we received the application fee from you."

"Oh, well, that must have been a mistake. I'll send it right now." Easy fix. Phew.

"It's really too late at this point. All decisions have been made."

"What do you mean?"

"We don't consider applications without payment."

I hadn't even been considered? All the feeling left me, and I was cold. Numb. *No. This could not be happening.* "What about the waiting list? Couldn't I still be put on the waiting list?"

"I'm sorry, I wish you'd called sooner. All spots are slotted at this point, regular and waitlist."

This was my plan. Away from everyone, starting new. I

mean, except Sam. Maybe I should be happy I was going to be closer to Sam. "There has to be something I can do."

"Reapply for spring semester—that's really it."

"Wouldn't you have wondered why someone would send in an application and not a fee?"

"Such is life, dear," she said softly. "We can't keep track of everyone who doesn't follow the guidelines. That's up to you."

"Of course, I'm sorry." I wanted to shout, though, that I was a girl who did follow guidelines. That everyone made a mistake once in a while and it shouldn't derail their future. "Well, um, thank you," I added. Hanging up, I pressed my trembling hands together to try and make them stop.

A knock on my bedroom door. My mother's thin face peering in. Her weak smile. "Was that Washington University?" she asked.

"They didn't get the application fee." I narrowed my eyes at her as a realization chilled my bones even further. "Did you not pay it?"

"What are you talking about?" she asked.

"I'm talking about when I gave you my computer to pay it."

"I thought I paid it. Of course, I thought I paid it."

The pressure was building behind my eyes, and I let out a bitter laugh of disbelief. Not because I couldn't believe it, but because I could, and I should've seen it coming. "Or you didn't on purpose."

"On purpose?" she echoed. "You really think I'd do something like that on purpose?"

I unraveled my legs and stood up. "You don't want me to go. You keep begging me not to go. What an easy solution! 'Don't worry Marin, I'll take care of it, don't bother your dad, I'll make sure it gets done'—*but then you didn't do it!*"

"Shouldn't you have double-checked it was paid? Wouldn't you have gotten an email if it wasn't? Can't you see on the portal if you didn't finish all the steps?"

"I don't know! When do I check my email?"

"You truly think I would do that to you, on purpose?" she whispered.

We stared at each other a moment and I realized that I really did. She was a desperate human. Desperate to save herself, to keep herself, to soothe herself. Whatever she'd wanted to know about my life, it was for her sake, to feel like a mother who'd been confided in. Whatever she'd wanted me to accomplish, it was for her sake, because then she could believe she had a hand in creating me. And whatever she'd wanted in our relationship, it was for her sake, so I could fill some sick need inside her. Our fights boiled down to her ego and how I didn't cater to it enough. I didn't love her enough. I didn't need her enough. I didn't want her enough.

But a one-way street didn't lend itself to getting what you wanted. And I was feeling about done. My chest was tightening. Hardening. Growing a cage and spikes. The scarce connection threading between us, already unraveling, snapped as the sharp blades of iron closed tight around me. "Yes, I really think you would."

She fell back against the doorframe. "What that says about our relationship, Marin—oh, God." And with a fistful of knuckles to her mouth, she sprouted tears. "Is there any hope for us?"

Brushing past her, I ran down the stairs.

She hurried after, her voice high. "We need to talk about this, Marin. You can't just walk out." She stopped on the bottom landing and held onto the rail, shuddering like a hailstorm was rushing through and around her.

A hailstorm, because her tears may as well have been ice for all she actually cared about me. "I can," I said, snatching my keys. "And I will."

She flew at me and grabbed my arm. I tried to wrench myself away, but she came with, and I couldn't keep it in anymore. As the first tears hit my face, she offered me a small, sad smile. "See? It's upsetting to you, too. That means there's hope for us still."

But I was stronger than her—*I would be stronger than her*—and I tried again, this time successfully ripping my arm from its socket and leaving it with her.

Or, at least, that's what it felt like.

She tried again, holding out a hand like she wanted to stroke my hair, but couldn't quite connect because I was too far away.

Like a rewind button had been pressed, all my misery got sucked back in and sealed up, so I could stand before her, sculpted smooth of emotion and dried arid. Her hand sprang back and curled into her chest as the dry ice worked its way through me, burning anything that might touch it.

Yes, I was long overdue in battening the hatches. And it was important she knew both the truth: "These aren't tears of hope, Mom," and believed the lie, "and they aren't for you."

My laptop was at my dad's, so that's where I went first. He wasn't home and the house felt empty, hints of my mother overtaking me and crawling up my skin—from the carpet she'd installed over the wood in my room when I was crawling out of my crib to the kitchen chairs she'd found purposely unmatched at garage sales to the stained glass she'd brought home from an art fair years ago and hung in the window over the sink.

It loomed large from where I sat at the kitchen table, as if a piece of her torn soul was hovering there, waiting for a victim.

My dad hadn't touched a thing in all this time. What was he holding onto? Or why was he so lazy to leave her contaminating the house like this? I ripped the small glass ornament off its hook and tossed it in the garbage. If I were him, I'd have gutted the house and remodeled, razed the landscaping and reseeded, whatever it took.

Settling back at the table, I vowed to find a solution.

KU was my only logical choice for next year, but I pulled up the Wash U website, anyway. That was what my hope was for. The way I figured it, there was only so much to go around, and I was hoarding mine not for my mother, but for myself and my life and my dreams.

How could I get closer to them, to Wash U, which I was so certain had been the right start? Away from my mom and Hannah and the world I'd grown up compromising myself inside.

Desperate for anything, I almost signed up for a summer engineering getaway. Stay at the dorms for a week, work together with other bright young minds...or a med-school club. Physical therapy was a version of medicine, right? Only, that was a meeting every week and a get-together every month. I'd have to drive four hours there and back, which would be kind of ridiculous, even if I was starting to ache for the solitude.

No, I wouldn't cry. She couldn't touch me.

I clicked over to the list of majors, to the list of schools, to physical therapy and then specializations. My eyes fell on *dance injuries*.

Dance. Wasn't Wash U known for its dance school, too? Scrambling, my fingers almost ripping the keys off the keyboard with their vehemence, I pulled up their dance programs.

And right there, a solution.

Closing my laptop as Sam knocked on the front door, I greeted him with an announcement: "I'm all signed up for a summer dance program. Take that, Elizabeth."

An entire summer.

She wanted to keep me here as long as she could? She wanted me within a comfortable, penned-in radius? Well, let's see what she had to say about me leaving in four months instead of seven, and how she felt about losing the last summer of my childhood.

Sam drew me against him. "I missed the cheering-you-up part, then?"

I'd texted him an SOS, and he'd promised to stop by on his way to work.

"No, I'm still very bitter," I admitted. "But at least I did something about it."

"What happened?" he asked.

"My mom may or may not have purposely derailed my Wash U application."

"Your mom wouldn't do that, would she?"

"The fact that it wouldn't surprise me is enough, don't you think?"

"Well, it definitely says something."

I frowned. "That's what she said."

"What are you going to do then? Go to KU with Hannah and Jon?"

"I'm sorry." I turned and led him down the hall to the kitchen. "I'd go to K-State if it didn't mean loans."

"Hey, it's closer than Wash U. Tell me about the summer thing."

My scowl brightened. "It's at Wash U, actually. Sort of an in, I figured, even though I wasn't originally planning to do a dance major. They have a good program, so who knows? It's been a long time since I did any serious technique or stretched like a ballerina, but maybe if I can hang with the other participants this summer, maybe I'd think about it. I used to want to be a dancer."

As I hopped up to sit on the kitchen counter, Sam stuttered to a stop in the middle of the room.

"But then you grow up, and people talk like that's silly, and you forget it could ever be a real option, you know? Not that I'm even thinking Broadway or L.A., but maybe Imani would let me come back and teach—she still sends me birthday cards. Or maybe I could own my own studio someday."

But Sam was still, like a snapshot, his face creased and fettered.

"What's wrong?" I asked.

He shook his head, but not in the way that meant *nothing*.

More like he needed a minute.

"You think it's silly? I mean, I'm not closing the door on physical therapy or anything. I don't have to decide now, not yet. You're right. I'm probably not good enough. Maybe I could have been, but..."

He cleared his throat like he wanted my attention, so I closed my mouth and motioned for him to come closer.

He started forward, slowly. "You're a better dancer than you give yourself credit for." Stopping at my knees, where he'd normally slide up between them, he added, "If I can see the difference, anyone can."

"Then what's wrong? Did I do something wrong?"

"It just hit that you're leaving earlier than planned."

"But this is better. We'll only be an hour and a half from each other next year."

"Next year. But now we don't have a summer together." He finally stepped into me then. "This isn't about me, right?"

I took his face in my hands. "Absolutely not. It's about everything and everyone else. If there's one thing right in my life, it's you. You're the only person I don't want to get away from, and the only one who will make it hurt."

He watched me with that Sam gaze of his, the one I felt viscerally, like tips of feathers probing soft and deep. I sat in it, let him discover what there was available to discover, and relaxed only when he leaned in. Right before he kissed me, he whispered, "Okay, then."

After Sam left for work, I went to the drugstore by myself.

On top of the numbing shock over what my mother might have done, there was the exhilaration of taking action and plowing ahead anyway, and the bitterness of losing a summer with Sam, which hadn't even crossed my mind in the frenzy I'd been in. All that, plus the hung-time continuum inside the old store, meant I couldn't tell for sure if it was my fault, the collision that resulted when someone came careening out of the aisle and smashed into me in front of the ice cream machine. Bags of candy collided with the floor and the empty cone in my hand landed with a soft crackle.

"Ugh, I'm *so* sorry," Whitney said, crouching down to scoop up the fallen cone. "I always assume no one else is in here."

"It's okay," I said, bending over to gather her candy. "Wow. Stockpiling for a nuclear war?"

"Not at all." She mocked offense. "Sugar is one of the six food groups."

I laughed as she tossed my cone. "It also causes inflammation."

"You've clearly been listening to your mom too much."

"Yeah, yeah." I waved her off as we walked to the counter with her bags. "Really, though, what do you need so much candy for?"

"Celebration." She looked at me, eyes bright. "I got the job, thanks to you."

"Oh, I'm sure that barely helped. You were always easy to talk to."

"Yeah?"

"Yeah."

"Three twenty-seven," the old man announced.

"That can't be right, Ernie," Whitney said. "No way a girl can buy ten bags of candy for three twenty-seven."

"In here you can," he insisted. "For my best customers, I charge cost only."

"Gotta keep yourself in business, though." She handed him a ten and grabbed her bag, then backed up before he could reach her with change.

"I owe for two cones, Ernie." How had I never known his name, in all these years? "I'm going to make another on the way out."

"Previous customer is paying it forward," he insisted, backing up the same way Whitney had.

With a sigh, I stuffed a dollar into the lolly canister, made myself a cone, and found Whitney waiting for me by the door. "Do you think that's really cost?" she whispered as we waved goodbye to Ernie and snuck out.

"Maybe in 1977," I replied.

She laughed. "They are a little gummy sometimes. You know, like if you left them out in the sun too long?"

"Or like they're as old as 1977?"

"Exactly."

"So where are you celebrating?" I asked.

She shrugged a quick shoulder. "Pre-gaming, I suppose you could say. My boyfriend's busy at the moment."

"I was celebrating by myself, too," I admitted.

"Got into your dream school?" she asked, only a little snide. Yeah, I guess to her I was the golden child.

"No, actually. But that's a long story." I stared at her for a minute, then glanced over at the library lawn, almost able to see shadows of us chasing each other around the triple trunk of the oak tree. Faster and faster, as fast as we could until we'd fall, dizzy, to watch the helicopters drift down onto us. Hannah had been too cool for that. She'd sat on the bench and licked her cone. "Want to celebrate together?" I asked, before I could think too much about it.

Looking over to the same place, eyes recalibrating to the kind of distance mine had been, she grinned. "Only if you tell me the long story."

"I will if you tell me about the boyfriend."

Then, without any more discussion, as if we'd done this too many times before to need explanation, we marched across the street, zipped our coats up all the way to keep out the cold, and took our usual spots.

Chapter 22

...or found.

I FOUND THE LETTER in my mom's old mail. The one she set aside to deal with later. The unimportant pile. But it was addressed to me, from Chapman. Fisting it, feeling the slice of corners in the crook of my thumb and center of my palm, I stormed downstairs to the kitchen where she was drinking tea.

Dropping it in front of her, letting it splash to the table so she could feel the spatter of my anger as it hit the wood, I said, my voice low and even, "You keeping something from me?"

She rested her palm on it and gave me sad eyes, an apologetic frown, and misery vibes.

No, not this again. This time it was about me, and there was no way she could turn it around. "I can't believe you'd keep something from me when you know how badly I want it. You think you can stop me from getting out of here?"

Her forehead creased and her head tilted sideways like a curious bird. Then, as she got what I was saying, her eyes went large. "Oh, Marin, this isn't what you think."

"What do I think? What isn't it?" I crossed my arms and dared her with an expletive that had her doing something impossible to herself.

"Really? You think I'd keep an acceptance letter from you?"

What other reason would she have to hide something from me, unless it was something that would get in the way of what she wanted?

Pressing her lips tight, she held my gaze. There was no frightened, guilty averting of eyes, and her face was soft, sympathetic rather than apologetic. Not like she, herself, was sorry for something. Not that she'd ever truly been that.

I looked down at it, though, hidden beneath her hand, and reassessed due to these slightly altered conditions. "Just because it's small, that doesn't mean... Mom, they do everything electronically these days. They're not going to send me a huge packet."

She released it, leaving it in the middle of the table for me to take. "Okay, sure."

"How can you know?"

This time she looked away. "Hold an envelope over steam for a bit and the seal just falls apart."

"You read my mail?"

"Better than your diary."

"I don't have a diary."

She looked back at me with barely a smile. "Because if

you did, you know I'd read it."

I sat down and ran both palms along the worn, soft maple. The sun was low and bright in the window. I squinted, and she went to lower the blinds.

We both watched the envelope on the table between us, now falling under thin slats of light and looking like a death sentence.

My mom reached her fingertips out, only the pads of them touching my arm. "You really think I'd do that to you?" she asked, her voice flooded and eyes brimming.

Yes, I did. But it didn't matter if she hadn't.

There was no doubt that, in every situation with me or my dad or anyone she'd come into contact with, she had blinders on and all she could see was herself. Honestly, I didn't think she could help it. I didn't think she was evil, or mean, or even selfish—not exactly. She was just impossibly near-sighted, the blinders giving sight only to how things affected her. Self-absorbed as the ultimate self-protection. So, yes, to protect herself from losing me, I could see her doing just about anything. I mean, when had she ever protected me in the past? Aside from physically as a toddler, obviously, since I was still here, what had I ever needed her protection from but herself?

"Marin?" she prodded, her eyes drying a bit in the waiting.

I shook my head. "It doesn't matter, Mom."

She clasped a hand to her chest. "It matters to me."

"Right now, what matters is this envelope." And we stared at each other. Here was the tipping point: would she let me be in this place I needed to be? Or would she yank me into her boxing ring?

For once, though, my face didn't feel hardened into cement. It was pleading with her, and I was vulnerable. Would she strike, or could I open my letter?

"Are we that broken?" she whispered, the tears gathering again and spilling over silently.

With a deep breath, I pulled the envelope to me and stood. I wouldn't do this here, then.

"No! Okay, okay. Stay, and we can talk about it later."

Her bangs trembled from a strong upward gale of breath, and I sat.

Focused. Zoning in. Nothing but me and my fate. I slid a finger against the flap, and it came apart easily. Hardly connected. My mom leaned forward over her mug, bobbing her tea bag up and down in the liquid like she was trying to power an engine, or power down her instincts to attack me about our relationship. As I studied the paper, smoothing it flat, I heard her lift the tea bag up and out and splat on the saucer.

I scanned it: *Dear Ms. Greene, Due to many qualified submissions and a limited number of spots... We regret to inform you... Though your name has been put on the waitlist, please don't be discouraged from applying again next year.*

A flood of ice glaciered through me, settling heavy on

my chest and pushing, pushing, holding me down. Folding my arms, I sank my cheek onto my hands as an ice pick smashed through my chest and shattered the hope I'd been letting myself hold onto.

"They made a terrible mistake," my mom muttered. "Awful decision-making skills. We should write them a strongly worded letter."

I snorted.

"Also, they shouldn't regret to inform you if you're on the waitlist. They should congratulate you for being on the waitlist. That's actually really been bugging me."

Moving my chin to my arms, I looked up at her. "This is all I want, Mom."

"Then you shouldn't stop reaching for it."

I put my cheek back down and closed my eyes.

"I called about the waitlist. Where you're at, it's not likely you'll make it in this year, but you should try again after the semester. And they told me about this dance program one of their instructors is doing at Wash U this summer. I looked it up, and Wash U is known for their dance major, too. Even if KU is your first stop, it doesn't have to be your last."

Breathing even, in and out—steady, steady, stay steady—I waited for a controlled moment to reply. "I don't know, Mom. Maybe you're right. Physical therapy is sensible, and helping dancers with injuries wouldn't be so bad. Maybe Imani would let me come back and help choreograph the solos on the side. Maybe that would be enough."

"You can start down both paths, Marin, and decide later. Anyway, I signed you up. The woman said the spots would go fast and I didn't want you to miss out. I hope that's okay."

Not steady, I squeezed my eyes tighter, a sometimes sufficient dam. Minutes ticked by. I had been so wrong. She not only didn't keep an acceptance letter from me, but she signed me up for something only I could want. The flood of confusion this brought sent cracks rippling out from the pressurized contents of my soul.

It felt like release. Like one ray of sunlight after an interminably gray winter reminding you to breathe. Like I'd been holding my breath around her for who knows how long and suddenly I realized maybe I didn't have to.

"Thanks, Mom," I finally managed to whisper.

Thanks, Mom? When had I ever said that before? And more importantly, when had I ever meant it?

I texted Sam before I left for the park. It was cold, but not wet, and not unbearable. Besides, right now I wanted to freeze off as many layers as I could, until they peeled away and left me raw.

We were supposed to hang out with his friends tonight. With Hannah. Me and Hannah. At this point, though, I didn't think I could stand it. Entering her world, even for Sam's sake, would take some kind of fortitude I did not think even a treasure hunter could find in me right now.

He hadn't replied to my text, but like any stellar boyfriend, he was waiting in the parking lot when I pulled in.

"You look really smart in glasses," Sam said, as I burrowed into him for a hug.

I smiled into his shirt, then up at him. "I should maybe teach you some better pick-up lines."

"Why would I need better pick-up lines?" he asked, as I headed for the park bench.

"Why not?"

Squeezing between two huge evergreens, each bigger than a house, I didn't notice his horror until we were on the other side.

He put a hand on my arm to stop me and turn me to him. "Marin, who will I be picking up?" His voice was steady, but his eyes were not. They were wide and hopping, searching, crawling. Spiders and earwigs and those miserable millipedes.

I shook them off. "You don't think you're going to meet any girls in college?"

"No. I planned to be too busy calling my girlfriend, and

texting my girlfriend, and visiting my girlfriend."

"Okay, Sam, calm down, it was just something I said."

"Didn't we just have this great moment the other day where I told you we'd be together forever?"

I stepped closer, trying to bring him back by grabbing the bottom of his coat. "Of course, forever works."

"Of course?" He yanked away from my grasp. "Were you just humoring me?"

"No!" I reached out again, but dropped my hands when I felt the cold front sweep in and blow me back.

They were just words, I wanted to cry. *I didn't know what I was saying!*

"Forever is amazing, but I don't think in forever. I'm only looking at the next few months before I leave."

"The next few months?" he echoed. "It's only February."

Wincing, I unloaded on him: the rejection, the summer program, the ultimate college decision. I would be going to KU.

"KU is way closer than Wash U." He was now stiff and brittle. "I could visit *for the day,* and you still assumed we'd break up?"

"No! *Please.* Forget I said anything."

"How am I supposed to forget you said anything?" After an inhale and exhale, he more calmly added, "I need a minute. And I have to go to work." He spun away and disappeared between the trees.

Staring after him for a moment—*What had just hap-*

pened?—I heard his truck start up.

No.

Hurrying back to the lot, I flung the passenger door open and slid in. "Sam. It wasn't that I planned on us breaking up. I don't *want* to. I don't want anyone else, and I'm not looking for anyone else."

Putting his hands on the steering wheel, he stretched his arms straight and dropped his head back. "You act like losing you is a foregone conclusion."

I had thought it was a foregone conclusion—he was right about that. Not because I wanted it to be, but because how many couples make it out of high school and into the real world?

"Just like a relationship is sometimes whatever it is no matter what you want it to be, a sentence is sometimes a bomb, no matter if you mean it that way." He said this softly, while looking out his driver's-side window.

"Sam, please."

"I need a minute, okay? I'll call you tomorrow." He refused to look at me, so I got out. The moment I closed the door, he backed up and drove off.

My eyes began to drip like a faulty faucet, and I slumped down onto the parking block in the space he'd left empty.

I'll call you tomorrow? What about after work, what about "meet me out back"? What about "I'll see you tonight"? Or even, "I'll see you later." So many better options.

Shit. What about hanging out with Hannah and his

friends? *Was I uninvited?*

The cold cement was numbing my butt, so I stood and got in my car. Maybe I didn't even have the fortitude for a February park bench. Maybe I needed the warmth and magic that had bolstered me the first time my world had fallen apart.

That was how I ended up standing in front of the ice cream machine by myself, wondering how many inches of cone I needed to stuff my face numb. Maybe I shouldn't have left the park. Had the snow not been melted, I could have simply laid face-down on the ground and that would've done the job.

"Hey!" Hannah's voice drifted from the deep, distant past and into my ear, but then she touched my shoulder, and I realized it wasn't the past.

"Oh, hey."

"You okay?" And that one look was all it took to remember what it felt like to be her friend. The concern that pulled her smile down over her teeth and the way her eyes seemed to draw closer when her forehead crinkled.

I blinked. Blinked again. It would have worked; the tears would have stayed away had she not reached out and pulled me into her. Silky cushions of coconut hair surrounded me, and I lost it, folding and breaking until tears slipped down my face.

At least I wasn't sobbing, or shaking, or out of control. At least it was more like dripping glass on a smooth surface.

At least I was reasonably still. Not still enough that she couldn't tell, though, because only when I'd gathered my composure completely did she let me go. And without direct eye contact, or even glancing at my face, she turned to the machine with a bright uptick to her voice. "How many inches do we need to fix it?"

"Ten," I replied, with what I hoped was a graceful sniffle.

She raised an eyebrow and looked at me. "Ten?"

"I mean, if you can get it that high."

She let out a short laugh. "Oh, don't go daring me like that. You might end up with a foot."

"I'm ready for a foot."

"I have to see this," Ernie said, immediately and spontaneously next to her on the other side.

"Are you a vampire, by any chance?" she asked, steadying her hand and placing her palm on the lever. "You move like a vampire."

"No fangs." He slipped his dentures out of place and then back in. "Not even any teeth."

Hannah looked back and forth between us. "All right. I'm going to need to concentrate for this one."

"Should I lock the door?" Ernie asked.

"Does anyone but us come in here?"

He looked put out. "This place has a constant stream of singular customers."

"Of course it does," I soothed. It would. Somehow, that made perfect sense. The magic of having a special place all to yourself, units of connected people the only ones able to enter at a time—if anyone could pull that off, it was Ernie. He might not be a vampire, but he was something.

"Okay, ready?" Hannah asked again, waiting for us both to nod. Then she began, slow and steady. Even the dust motes hung in the air so as not to disturb the balance. We didn't breathe, or twitch, or sniff, or allow our hearts to beat. Time suspended to bolster the creation of a masterpiece.

Fatter than normal, to support the height—she'd always been shit for math but somehow knew the ratio needed for a stable ice cream cone—she finished as quick as she'd started slow. Turning around at a snail's pace, one hand out and ready to catch it should it fall, she held it out to me, a tower of numbing comfort, which I almost didn't feel like I needed anymore.

Ernie clapped. "That one"—he nodded—"is definitely on the house."

"Wait!" Hannah put a palm up and reached in her pocket for her phone. "Let me take a picture."

"I'll take it, of both of you," Ernie said, grabbing her cell before she could reply.

She looked at me, the barest question in her glance, and I nodded, the slightest tip of my head. Then, beaming with an ice cream cone as big as our heads, we took our first picture together in at least three years.

Ernie slid back into place behind his counter, and Hannah and I walked to the door. When we got there, neither of us made a move to leave.

"Wanna talk about it?" she asked, her attention flitting to the cone.

"I didn't get into Chapman, and Sam and I got in a fight." I shoved ice cream in my mouth before I could elaborate.

She sat on the ledge of the big front windows. It was low and narrow, clearly not comfortable, but I joined her and unloaded—there was no end to this store's magic.

"You have to call him," she insisted as I finished.

"He's at work."

"Then text him, or go there."

"What would I say? I already apologized."

"Give me your phone."

"Um, no."

"Give me your phone or I'll knock that cone to the floor."

"You would never."

"I would." And she yanked my cell from my back pocket.

"Hey!" I cried. Which is what she typed to him, but without the exclamation point.

hi, he replied immediately.

Her hair brushed my cheek as we bent over her lap where she worked my phone with her fingers. **i cant wait until tomorrow to fix this**

"We're not supposed to be on our phones at work," I pointed out.

"Well, he was obviously waiting for you."

>**me either**, he replied. **sorry i left like that**

no<

im sorry<

things happened really fast today<

my mom signed me up and i cant not go<

its what I want for my life<

you know?<

"Wow," I nodded, in the midst of licking ice cream drips. "It's like you're inside my head."

Then she added:

trust me<

id rather spend every minute of the summer with you<

id rather drink you in so I c

"No," I said, scrambling for the phone.

She held it up, as far from me as she could. "Tell me you don't feel that way."

And I was slammed with memories of her round penmanship on pink paper splashed with perfume. All the love notes she'd written for boys in elementary and middle school, which she'd crafted for the three of us, most of which never made it out of the house.

"I do feel that way, but I want it to be my words, not yours. We're not in middle school anymore."

She studied the phone, as if she wasn't sure I was grown enough to handle this task that she'd always been in charge of. Then she deleted what she'd written and handed it over to me.

you can come with in my pocket or my suitcase or my trun

"No." With a palm to her face, she shook her head. "You sound like a serial killer. Try again."

But I was getting melted ice cream all over my phone, so I handed it back to her. "You're only typing for me," I instructed. "Say, *I wish you could come with. We are so much more than I thought we could be.*"

Her aura went quiet, a thing that only seemed noticeable with a girl like her, and I had to remember she'd liked him, too. But she typed it and hit send. A hung moment, and then:

>you promise?
>there's no part of you that's waiting to leave me
>that wants a change or someone else

This time I traded her, the phone for the cone.

god no<
you know how I feel about relationships<

what a waste of time<

In Hannah's defense, she objected to this but I was too quick for her.

um<

except you<

you make it all worth it<

With this, she nodded and smiled proud, then looked away and gave us our privacy, which made me feel like I'd earned something. Respect? Approval?

>we still on for tonight

>or are you not up for a party

I glanced at Hannah, her whole body turned away from me now. She was tapping her foot to an old song Ernie had playing, and I vaguely remembered some choreography we must have been taught when we were younger.

ill meet you after work<

>i really want to kiss you again, he replied, an echo of our beginning and something he said to me randomly now, even though I'd said it first.

With a grin, I typed his original response: **i really want you to go to the dance with me**

Staring at the words for a bit, an idea formed in my head. After everything he'd done, it made sense that I would ask him. To a dance. Officially.

Pushing send, I stood and shoved my phone in my pocket. "Hey Hannah, wanna go to the florist with me?"

"Time heals what reason cannot."

—*Seneca*

...After

THE LAST PICTURE I had of us was from the day I left for the summer dance program.

We were standing near that same stretch of sidewalk, arms around each other again. Hannah's smile matched her giant top-knot, while Whit's thin lips curled out something mysterious, her long form only made longer now with her waist-length hair. Sam was the only one in the picture not looking at the camera. He was looking at me instead.

My hair was down, and a few strands lifted in the wind, while my face—and my smile—was easy, open, and bright.

Having them both together again made me feel whole.

"When we see you next, your nose will be pierced, right?" Whit asked. She and Hannah had bonded over this recent graduation celebration of theirs, but I hadn't caved yet.

I glanced at Sam, who was driving me to Wash U and staying the weekend while I got settled. "Sam and I are getting matching ones as soon as we get there."

He chuckled as my mom gaped at us. She'd taken the picture. "You are not coming back with a hole in your face."

"Don't worry, it's going to be the smallest stud they have. Those teeny-tiny silver ones you can hardly see."

"Nothing like ours," Hannah said. They both had little hoops—Hannah's gold and Whit's silver.

My mom drew a big intake of air. "That will completely ruin your wedding photos."

"Not if we both have them," Sam pointed out, playing along with my joke.

"It's not like I'm getting a neck tattoo," I said.

"Oh God, Marin, *are you getting a neck tattoo?*" My mom looked back and forth between my two best friends. "Is nose piercing code for neck tattoo?"

"If she gets a neck tattoo," my dad said, coming out of the house with the last box, "I'm not paying for college, wherever she is."

"Well, we can agree on that," my mom muttered.

I drew my mom into a hug—a real one—while she twitched a little. "I'm not getting a neck tattoo," I promised. "Calm down."

She started sniffling when I let her go, and I moved to my dad, then Hannah and Whitney, both at once, like we'd never split up in the first place. "Take care of each other while I'm gone," I muttered, so soft they might not have heard me. And maybe they didn't, because they didn't reply. Or maybe they did, but it was just a little soon for them to admit they might want to.

Squeezing Sam's hand on my way around the car to the passenger seat, I bit my lip to stop the tears. I'd wanted freedom and distance more than anything, and I wanted my life to turn out my way, but now felt too soon.

Everything had just started working out for me, and already I was walking away. I could only hope it would all be the same when I got back.

Hope. The word shuddered through me. Sometimes it was all you had. And sometimes, it was enough.

Acknowledgments

This story, previously known as EITHER/OR, was one of the first manuscripts I finished. Authors and editors I no longer remember deserve to have their names in these acknowledgements, due to their words of encouragement and the wisdom they lent along the way. I feel like an entirely different author now, from the one who brought this with shaky hands to her first writer's conference in New York City close to fifteen years ago.

What that means is that everyone mentioned in previous acknowledgments (and then some) should also be included here, as the odds are good they critiqued this one as well: Kat, Paul, Angie, Moy, Mary, Rochelle, Karla, Nancy, and Jeff. That's not to forget Jenn, Judy, Claire, Michelle, Aimee, Ashley, and like I said, more whose names have fallen into the black hole that is my mind.

Thank you also to my newest writer friends who inspire me every time I lay eyes on their work, and who push me to keep moving forward. Beth Stedman, Sarah Zimmerman, and Kieran Lamoureux — drafting with you has been enriching, motivating, and a complete delight. You literally showed up right when I needed you. Beth, you've created my new favorite thing with this group you dreamed up.

And finally, thank you to Aurielle, for coming along on the ride and then jumping in the deep end with me. It's so nice to have you here.

Other young adult by J Mercer

The Shady Woods Series

Perfection and Other Illusive Things

Triplicity

Please consider leaving a review for
IN ONE LIFE AND OUT ANOTHER.
Reviews and word-of-mouth make all the difference!

Perfection and Other Illusive Things

I hid the school newspaper from my best friend.

Billie wouldn't appreciate that I wasn't reading the *news* part of it, and she'd roll her eyes when she realized it was Hawk's words I was melting over. *Him again?* she'd say. *Honestly, Eden. He's going to be working at a gas station for the rest of his life.*

Except we didn't even know if he worked at a gas station in the first place. Her point, of course, was that I wasn't the type of girl to date a guy who'd end up in a job like that. My point, if I actually felt like having the conversation, was that his words were perfection and clearly he was more of an intellect than she took him for.

Mr. Keller clapped and I startled, crumpling the paper in my hands. I resisted the urge to smooth it on my thigh and draw attention to the fact that I wasn't listening in class, because, you guessed it, I also wasn't the type of girl to not listen in class.

"Your semester project will, of course, end with a thoughtful essay—psychology applied, if you will—but for starters I just want you to pick something, preferably something you don't like very much, and make a list of pros and cons for it. I'm going to give you some time to work on this, and then we'll get into the details later—what the next step will be. Sound good? As it's a large part of your grade, make sure you put a little thought into it."

Something I didn't like very much? But everything I wasn't supposed to like, I did like: Hawk's poems, Hawk himself, the watch my grandpa gave me right before he died…it had been my grandma's and this morning, in the drizzle that he loved, I'd almost put it on. Then I heard Billie's words in my ear: "Watches are obsolete." And my mom's: "That old thing? Does it even work?"

It did, actually. Well, sometimes. When it wanted to. But even if it didn't, I'd still love it. It was gold and vintage and delicate.

When I put it on, though, I was reminded of how *not* delicate I was. Not that strong, independent girls like me were supposed to want to be delicate. Strong and sturdy made for good volleyball players, and I was supposed to care about what my body could do, not what it looked like.

And no, I didn't want to be delicate only because Hawk's best friend Ivy was ethereal. Or because the girls he went for were usually as thin as her. A girl like me didn't have a chance with a guy like him anyway. Or, as Billie would put it, a guy like him didn't have a chance with a girl like me.

Frankly, I was pretty sick of being a girl like me.

Girls like me did what they were supposed to, that's what I'd come to realize. Not what they wanted. Girls like Ivy did what they wanted, and, it seemed to me, seldom what they were supposed to. There had to be a happy medium. There had to be an in-between.

The bell rang and I stuffed the crumpled paper into my pocket.

"What are you doing your list on?" Billie asked, collecting her stuff from the desk next to mine.

"My grandma's watch." It was the only thing in my head. It just came out.

"You're supposed to pick something you don't like. Were you even listening?"

"No one else likes it, though. Maybe my pros will convince them."

"Wes likes it."

I refrained from rolling my eyes. "Wes likes everything."

She winked. "Wes likes everything to do with you."

Yeah, yeah, I wanted to say. A girl like me would date a guy like Wes. Only, Billie and I had been best friends with him and Isaac for so long that when he'd kissed me three months ago, it felt more like kissing my grandpa. And when we managed to still act like best friends the next day, it seemed better that way.

See, I had everything a girl like me should want: stellar grades, early admission to my third-choice college, a solid spot on the volleyball team, the most loyal best friend, the sweetest little brother, a mom who loved me, et cetera.

It wasn't that I didn't want those things; obviously, they were very nice things. It was just I wanted things outside that box too. Things Billie didn't understand. Things my mom wouldn't understand. Or Wes. Obviously, because he thought I should want him. So if I didn't want the things a girl like me should want, then maybe I wasn't really that girl anymore. And what was I supposed to do with that?

Maybe I should do my project—the pros and cons—on me.

Maybe I should do it on the girl I was supposed to be.

9 798987 256732